monsoonbooks

DIRTY OLD MEDIA MEN

Millie Lee (pseudonym) works in the Singapore media.

Praise for *Dirty Old Media Men*

'A journalist's exposé of journalism in Singapore … fun, funny and absolutely appalling! Filled with pithy irony, Millie Lee gives us much to think about in her graphic descriptions of a fictitious Singapore newsroom. Shocking!'

Devika Misra, *The Asian Bookshelf* and former 938Live broadcaster

'I absolutely love it! Beautifully crafted with hilarious characters. I laughed out loud so many times, my husband wants to read it now.'

Neo Swee Lin, actor

'A delightful read that invokes and provokes various emotions. A steely effort of grit and humour, shining the light on the underbelly of sexual harrassment in newsrooms.'

Braema Mathi, human rights activist, former Nominated Member of Parliament and *Straits Times* senior correspondent

Dirty Old Media Men

Millie Lee

monsoon

monsoonbooks

First published in 2024
by Monsoon Books Ltd
www.monsoonbooks.co.uk

No.1 The Lodge, Burrough Court, Burrough on the Hill,
Melton Mowbray LE14 2QS, UK.

First edition.

ISBN (paperback): 9781915310248
ISBN (ebook): 9781915310255

A Cataloguing-in-Publication data record is available from the British Library.

FSC www.fsc.org MIX Paper | Supporting responsible forestry FSC® C018072

Printed and bound in Great Britain by Clays Ltd, Elcograf S.p.A.
26 25 24 1 2 3

For my mother

‘*An educated woman is a worthless woman.*’
Confucius (allegedly)

'Telling me to relax or smile when I'm angry is like bringing a birthday cake into an ape sanctuary. You're just asking to get your nose and genitals bitten off.'

Amy Poehler, *Yes Please*

Contents

THE PROBATION

Part I: News Media

August – September

Day 1 – Morning

Peranakan Pervert kept staring at my cleavage. I'm Chinese. My cleavage is distinctly average at best, but the bra cup and the cut of my top accentuated my dullest features.

He was using my resumé as a shield, stealing glances over the top of it. 'Ah, national junior badminton champion,' he blurted out.

'Yes,' I muttered, pulling at the edges of my skirt.

'I used to play a bit of badminton myself.' Peranakan Pervert locked his fingers, turned his palms towards me and stretched his arms. The saggy flesh around his triceps wobbled. He leaned across the desk. 'Used to be the news desk champion.'

'Really?'

'Yeah, you can ask them.' He pointed enthusiastically through the glass partition that separated him from the other journalists, beavering away at their desks. 'You ask them.'

Peranakan Pervert really wanted me to ask them.

'I will.'

'Yeah.' He threw his hands behind his head, revealing both the underside of his pale, wobbly arms and clumps of armpit hair. 'You should.'

We had exhausted the topic of his conversation, but one of us hadn't quite realised it yet.

'That's why you're so fit,' he said.

'I'm sorry?'

'Your physique.' He was now drawing the outlines of my shoulders in the air. 'Your upper body strength.' He was now pointing at my breasts. 'You can tell you are an athlete.'

I shrugged. 'No more already.'

'What happened?'

'Er, too many injuries. Too much studying. I couldn't balance everything.'

'Well, you balanced your studies.' He waved my resumé in the air. 'First class honours degree in Mass Comm at NTU. That's impressive.'

'Thank you.'

Peranakan Pervert decided to look serious. He said, 'Why do you want to be a journalist?'

He ran a hand through his hair. He was in his late 50s, so it was thick and black and dyed.

I said, 'I've always wanted to be a writer.'

He leaned forward. 'But you know that you'll be expected to do much more than that, right? As section head, I'll be your overall supervisor for your six-month probationary period. But we'll expect you to work across all platforms. Online news. Radio. And then TV. Two months each one. And when you get confirmed, as I'm sure you will, we'll decide which area to focus on.'

'Sounds good,' I said.

'Of course, it doesn't really matter now. Cross-pollination is essential for any newsroom. It's quite possible you'll file a story for the website in the morning, promote it on news radio in the afternoon and then possibly do a piece to camera in the evening.'

'Sure.' I was eager to get started. Peranakan Pervert was rubbing his thighs too much.

He said, 'I think you'll do well on the TV side.'

'Why?'

'You've got that ...' Peranakan Pervert waved a hand in front of his face. 'Look.'

'What look is that?'

'A TV look.' He pretended to read my resumé to hide his blushes. 'Your writing impressed your tutors though.'

I reiterated that I wanted to be a writer, rather than a TV presenter.

My supervisor said, 'Always good to have different options in the media though, not like me. I've got a face for radio.'

Peranakan Pervert laughed far too loudly so I chuckled politely, which seemed to upset him. I took it upon myself to cheer him up. I asked if he did much radio. 'Nah,' he said wistfully. 'Not since they put a camera in the studio.'

Peranakan Pervert insisted on giving me a personal tour of the newsroom. The high ceilings and windows made the place feel like Changi Airport during lockdown. Most of the desk cubicles were bare, except for the odd ethernet cable.

'It's very quiet,' I said.

'Most of the journalists are out on assignment,' my new supervisor said quickly.

I noticed that the journalists took their computers and files and personal belongings with them on assignments, leaving nothing at all behind.

'It's a state-of-the-art media complex, with a fully integrated newsroom. We can now house every news, radio, production and broadcast journalist under one roof,' he said proudly.

I pointed out that the place was almost empty.

Peranakan Pervert looked longingly around the vast, near deserted newsroom and said, 'Yeah, most work from home now.'

He cheered up when he spotted a balding Chinese man sitting alone at a cubicle, hunched over his computer. He said, 'Ah, our chief sub-editor never works from home.'

Peranakan Pervert led me by the arm, squeezing my bicep a little too tightly as we hurried past a row of empty desks. He said, 'Uncle Groper, meet the new girl.' Then to me, 'This man is a newsroom legend. Been here for at least thirty years.' Uncle Groper moved quickly to minimise all the tabs on his screen. He pushed his keyboard aside and opened a container of fishball noodles. He slurped loudly and beckoned me towards a swivel chair beside him. He slapped the chair hard and said, 'You're the new reporter, is it? What's your name?'

'Millie Lee,' I said, accepting the chair beside his BO.

'Wah, sounds like a movie star,' he said. 'You from which school?'

'NTU.'

'You work on their newsletter there?'

'Yeah, I was the editor in my final year.'

Uncle Groper almost choked on his soup. 'Wah, this one a scholar, is it?' Peranakan Pervert nodded, but Uncle Groper was clearly unimpressed. The old man said, 'Everyone a scholar now. Can you write a headline or not?' I thought I could so Uncle Groper tapped my knee with his sweaty hand. He said, 'No, can you write a *good* headline or not? Come. Look at this story.' He pointed a stubby finger at the screen. 'This one about public transport. Gonna be a fare review next year. Prices will definitely go up. For buses and trains. What's your headline?'

Without really thinking, I said, 'Er, I don't know. More pain on the train?' It wasn't a great headline. Just a short, silly rhyme. I knew that. But it was early in the morning and I wasn't expecting an early interrogation on sub-editing.

'No, cannot,' Uncle Groper snapped, tapping my exposed thigh this time. I was seriously regretting the skirt now.

He said, 'The headline is going to be "Bus and train fare structure to be reviewed". I was dumbfounded. Both men could see it, too.

At NTU, my editorship was built on a sense of camaraderie, openness and collective sharing.

I couldn't help myself. I said, 'Isn't that headline a bit ...'

'A bit what?' Peranakan Pervert asked.

'Well, a bit straight?'

Uncle Groper digested my question as he digested a whole fish ball. He made as much noise doing both. He said, 'Straight how?'

I said, 'It's your main story on the homepage, right? It's just a literal explanation of what's going to happen.'

Uncle Groper and Peranakan Pervert suddenly found me hilarious. '*Aiyah*, of course it's literal. It's a *gahmen* story,' said Uncle Groper. 'Just do what the *gahmen* says they will do. Save your puns for the silly stories and you'll be fine.' The old man squeezed my thigh this time. 'Good luck, Millie Lee.' He didn't shake my hand, which was a blessing. His fingers were soaked in soup. And he had forgotten to close the porn tab on his computer.

Day 1 – Lunchtime

I went to lunch with Lauren Lam. She was an experienced news reporter and Peranakan Pervert had earlier suggested pairing me up with another woman. We met at a café across the road from the newsroom. She was also Chinese, but slightly older, probably in her late twenties and certainly wearier.

She was good company though. She listened intently to my atypical story. I told her all about my journey from a three-room flat to top PSLE results and then onto one of the best Catholic girls' schools in Singapore before ending up with a media scholarship.

She wanted to know who I'd met in the newsroom.

I said, 'Well, Peranakan Pervert, obviously. He's going to be my supervisor.'

She nodded. 'Yeah, he was mine when I was on probation. He's been there since he left school. Must be almost sixty now. Loves working with the younger ones.'

'Oh, and I met Uncle Groper,' I added, cornering a spoonful of rice on my plate.

'What did you get? Knee or thigh?'

'Both.'

Lauren smiled. 'Wah, he likes you then.'

I held the spoon to my mouth. 'Have you ever seen him watch ...'

'Porn? All the time. He's the original *ah pek*. Been scolded so many times already. Doesn't care. They think it's better he does it in the office, discreetly, rather than on the MRT.'

On the plus side, Lauren said he was a very good sub-editor.

She said, 'Uncle Groper has won headline of the year. Twice.'

She sensed my discomfort and started giggling. 'I'm serious. There was one about a couple who proposed in a Burger King at Plaza Sing. His headline was "I only have fries for you".'

'That is good,' I conceded, chewing the rice.

'It's better than his original headline.'

'What was that?

'Would you like to see my whopper?'

I spat the rice across the café table. 'Oh, shit. I'm so sorry.'

'It's fine,' said Lauren, handing me a tissue from her packet. 'Uncle Groper loves sex puns in his headlines. But then our older readers do too, especially the really puerile stuff. Most of them are Catholic school boys. Good English. Bad Mandarin. Lousy EQ.'

'Yeah, I suppose,' I said, wiping the last of the rice grains away.

Lauren gazed at me, watching me ball up the tissue. She said, 'Anyone try to shag you yet?'

Her unexpected question floored me. 'What? No, of course not.'

'Don't worry,' she said. 'They will.'

Day 1 – Afternoon

Peranakan Pervert made me accompany him to the evening conference, where the section heads gathered to discuss the major stories for the next day. I was invited into the room, but not allowed to sit at the long mahogany table. My new supervisor ushered me towards a chair placed against the far wall.

'Just observe,' he said. 'Tell me what you think over coffee later.' Peranakan Pervert smiled at me, revealing nicotine-stained teeth. He reminded me of an uncle on my father's side who only visited during Chinese New Year. He stank of stale cigarettes too.

I was used to it though. Many media and arts students smoked at NTU. They were creative people after all.

Mother Superior was the first to join us in the conference room. She was a middle-aged cross between Ursula from the *Little Mermaid* and Dustin from *Stranger Things*.

Mother Superior had previously worked for the Internal Security Department. Mother Superior had no previous journalism experience.

Mother Superior told experienced journalists how to write sensitive local copy. All local copy was sensitive in Singapore.

Mother Superior was still single. She was married to the job.

She dumped a stack of papers on the table. They were covered in red ink. She said, 'I swear these interns get worse every year.' She glared at me. 'You an intern?'

I shook my head.

'No *lah*, this is Millie Lee,' said Peranakan Pervert, sitting across from Mother Superior at the table. 'The one I told you about *lah*.'

'Can she write?'

'Don't know yet.'

'None of them can write anymore.'

Mother Superior took out a red pen and scrawled on the top sheet of paper. 'Cannot even rewrite a press release,' she growled. 'Made this one cry this morning.'

'*Aiyoh*, not again,' said Peranakan Pervert. 'Why?'

'Juxtaposition,' said Mother Superior. 'Had the word "*corrupt*" in the same paragraph as "*minister*".' Mother Superior scrunched up the paper.

Peranakan Pervert assumed the piece wasn't suggesting the minister was corrupt. Mother Superior said, 'Doesn't matter. Juxtaposition. Cannot.'

She threw the paper towards the wastepaper basket. She missed. No one moved to pick it up. The newsroom had underpaid foreign workers for that. I thought about picking up the paper myself when a whirlwind blew into the evening conference. Hokkien Half-Ball was only a few years older than me but dressed like a teenager. His hair was short and spiky. He was dressed in tight jeans and a Guns N' Roses T-shirt. He looked like a US skateboarder from the suburbs. He sounded like Ah Beng from Sembawang.

He even had a tattoo. A Chinese scholar with a tattoo was like a gay man in local politics. They had to exist, statistically, but I'd never met any.

Hokkien Half-Ball was also ridiculously laidback, for a Chinese guy, for a Singaporean, for an Aussie surfer even. He oozed self-assurance. He owned the room immediately.

'How can they concede a last-minute goal?' He threw up his hands. 'How? Basket.' He slumped into a seat beside Peranakan Pervert, who asked how much he'd lost. 'Too much.'

Hokkien Half-Ball spotted me, sitting at the back of the room. He smiled at me. It was a cheeky smile. He had good teeth. 'Hello.'

'Hello,' I croaked. My voice abandoned me. What the hell

was wrong with me?

'Ah, this is our lifestyle and commentary editor,' said Peranakan Pervert, slapping his much younger colleague on the shoulder. They were obviously friends. 'Used to be separate departments, but he was so talented they merged the two and gave him both.'

Mother Superior tutted. But she didn't look up. She had copy to eviscerate. Hokkien Half-Ball said, 'Balls *lah*. After the last retrenchment exercise, I was the only one left.' He was already on his feet, making his way around the long mahogany table. 'Welcome to the newsroom,' he beamed.

His handshake was warm, but slightly clingy. He held on a little too long, long enough for the sweat to come between our palms. 'Wah, you're very young ah? How old are you?'

I mumbled about being twenty-two, but almost twenty-three.

'First job, is it?'

'Yah.'

'Me, too. And somehow, I've not been fired yet.'

Hokkien Half-Ball was self-deprecating. I liked that.

'There's still time,' Mother Superior muttered. She was not self-deprecating. She looked up this time though, revealing her tight curly hair and now all I could see was Dustin from *Stranger Things*.

'You're still here,' said Hokkien Half-Ball, returning to his seat.

'I still do my job properly,' said Mother Superior, running a line through an entire paragraph.

'How many interns did you make cry this week?'

'Two.'

'Only two?' Hokkien Half-Ball folded his arms in mock disgust. 'It used to be many more at ISD, right?'

This time, Mother Superior did not look up. She did grimace though. Beneath the curls, she looked like a Cabbage Patch Kid. Her previous job had been with the Internal Security Department. It was an obvious stick to beat her with. Our editors and section heads often came from different government ministries or were handpicked scholars.

Our board members tended to come from the Singapore Armed Forces. They didn't know the rules of subject-verb agreement, but they did know the rules of engagement in the South China Sea, which must be useful tips to pass on to young writers.

Mother Superior decided to change the subject. She said, 'He's late again.'

'He's busy wha',' said Hokkien Half-Ball, scrolling through his phone. 'Hey, you think Man U one ball can ah?'

'Nah, not worth it,' said Peranakan Pervert.

I had no idea what they were talking about.

'I know who is worth it,' whispered Hokkien Half-Ball.

'Eh, cannot, I was first.'

'Too old already.'

I had no idea that they thought I was deaf either.

Slick Scholar silenced them. Slick Scholar silenced all of us. Even Mother Superior stopped brutalising a court report and lowered her red pen. They all looked towards him. I looked towards him. This was a near religious experience for me. It was close to being an orgasmic experience.

Slick Scholar was only thirty-three and a national editor already. He was like a weird mix of Mark Zuckerberg and the

Winklevoss twins. He was a fast-talking polymath who could still attract women. His first book of poetry was published before his A-Level results.

Some of it was even readable.

His degree came from Cambridge, the masters came from Harvard and the government approval came from the highest levels. He was the anointed one. He did the one-on-one interviews with cabinet ministers. He was involved with international foundations and advised think tanks. He sailed for Raffles Institution and Cambridge.

He was a real man of the people.

But he could write. He could really write. His columns on nationhood and what it meant to be a Singaporean genuinely inspired me. He was one reason why I was sitting at the back of the room. Now he was standing at the front of that same room. And he looked a bit like Henry Golding. That really didn't help matters. Eventually, I realised that he was staring at me. Everyone was staring at me. I was standing up.

No one else was standing up.

When he'd entered the room, my Catholic school default setting had returned and I'd scrambled to my feet, like I was ready to recite the national bloody pledge.

'Oh, hello, you must be Millie,' said Slick Scholar, slowly and smoothly. He knew my name. He interviewed prime ministers and presidents regularly, but he knew *my* name.

'Yes, I am, and you must be a sexy genius.'

That's what I thought anyway.

'Er, yeah ... yeah ... I'm, er, Millie ... Hello.'

That's what I actually said, trying to avoid the other smirking men in the room and a tut-tutting sociopath with a red pen.

'Well, come and join us at the table then,' said Slick Scholar, taking his seat.

Mother Superior dumped a stack of papers on the seat beside her. Hokkien Half-Ball pulled back the chair beside him. 'Come *lah*.'

I joined the men's side of the table. Peranakan Pervert appeared to be dribbling. On the other side, Mother Superior looked ready to stab me in the throat with her red pen.

Slick Scholar said, 'OK, I've got a meeting upstairs after this with Captain Mayhem. So I'll need to make this a quick one.'

Captain Mayhem is the CEO of our English media organisation. Captain Mayhem's first language is not English.

Captain Mayhem has no media training or experience. Captain Mayhem's previous career was spent entirely in the finance and banking sectors.

Captain Mayhem was hired to lead our transformation across all digital media platforms and to connect with the lost audience of Generation Z. Captain Mayhem is sixty-seven years old.

Captain Mayhem once thought that TikTok was an online version of noughts and crosses.

Captain Mayhem is the CEO of our English media organisation.

'Right, I'll go first,' said Hokkien Half-Ball. 'We've got an interview with the victim of the viral driver.'

Slick Scholar leaned forward. 'Which one?'

Hokkien Half-Ball said, 'That one *ah*, the one with the BMW.'

'The one who ran over the security guard?'

'No, the other BMW.'

'The one who drove through the bus stop to cut the queue?'

'No, the other one.'

'The one who *tekan* the bus driver?'

'No, the other one.'

'Which one? I can't keep up.'

'The one who gave a middle finger to the pedestrian.'

'That's it?'

'The pedestrian was a nine-year-old girl.'

'*Aiyoh*. Can she talk?'

'Can *lah*.'

'Are they both the same race?'

'*Yah lah*. I checked first.'

'OK, good. But is that it? That's your lead story?'

'The video got 1.2 million hits already. We want the demographic, right?'

'Fine. Better record a podcast as well then,' said Slick Scholar, checking his watch. 'What about you?'

He turned to Mother Superior. She shuffled her papers like a newsreader and picked a sheet from the top of the pile. 'The Government says inflation will continue to rise. The cost of living will increase. Prices will keep going up.'

'Hmm. So how?'

Mother Superior said, 'So we go with the angle that inflation will drop in the future and use a big, cute picture of the Mid-Autumn festival.'

'Very good. How is the National Day package coming along?'

'Er, excuse me.' I realised my hand was in the air.

Slick Scholar was taken aback initially. Then he grinned at me. 'Yes, Millie.' I felt the eyes of the others in the room, burning holes through my forehead.

'Nah, it's OK, I just wasn't sure of something. It's nothing.'

'Clearly, it's something for you. What's up?' Slick Scholar's voice was wasted on us. He should be reading inspirational audiobooks for a living.

I said, 'It's just that the current news is that inflation is going up today, right now, but our angle is going to be that inflation will go down, eventually, at some unknown time in the future.'

'God, they're getting worse,' hissed Mother Superior.

'No, it's a good point,' said Slick Scholar, adjusting his white shirt. 'But we've got to find the right balance.'

'For who?' I said.

'For *whom*,' Mother Superior corrected.

'For our readers,' Slick Scholar pointed out.

'I bet you fifty bucks I shag her by National Day,' Hokkien Half-Ball whispered.

'On,' Peranakan Pervert muttered, shaking hands with Hokkien Half-Ball below the table.

'But it is a good point, a really good point,' said Slick Scholar, sitting back, as if ruminating on something. He turned to Peranakan Pervert. 'Who's producing the National Day package?'

'I am,' said Hokkien Half-Ball.

'Great. Take Millie with you. Come up with a colour piece that she can write.'

'Sure.' Hokkien Half-Ball winked at me, before leaning into Peranakan Pervert's ear. 'Make it a hundred,' he whispered.

Day 1 – Night

I just woke from the most surreal dream. I was standing in front of thousands of flag-waving Singaporeans at the National Day Parade. I waved my notepad at them, trying to get their attention, but they kept singing Dick Lee's *Home* back at me instead.

A policeman tried to escort me from the stage. He removed his helmet to reveal that he was Hokkien Half-Ball. He winked at me and said: 'Is that a truncheon or am I just pleased to see you?'

He began to stalk me across the stage, pleading for a chance to show me his truncheon. I ran towards the crowd and shouted: 'He's trying to have sex with me!' 'No,' cried Mother Superior, rising from her seat in the VIP section. 'He IS trying to have sex with me! Never use contractions in your copy!'

Day 4

I had spent two days and nights reading up on previous National Day Parade coverage and still felt woefully underprepared. It didn't help that Hokkien Half-Ball was humming the melody of Dick Lee's *Home* as we drove to the Padang. I could only see him coming towards me with his truncheon. 'Don't worry *lah*,' he said, changing lanes and not signalling. 'It's the same every year. Big military display for Malaysia and some nice fireworks for TV. Just get some heart-tugging shit about "what it means to be Singaporean". And get some crying. Must have crying. After the last show, all the editors want crying.'

After an hour of trudging up and down the metal staircases of the temporary stands around the Padang, I realised that Singaporeans didn't really cry. My father has never cried, not in front of me anyway. He's a typically taciturn Singaporean male: hardworking, serious and largely incapable of public displays of emotion, unless he's sitting at a mahjong table on a Sunday afternoon. My mother cries when she's watching her favourite Chinese dramas, the ones with actors pretending to have special needs to win awards. But she's never wept in public.

And no one had the decency to sob at the National Day Parade either. Eventually, I tracked down an older Chinese guy wiping his eyes. He was in his early fifties and had voluntarily painted his face red and white – so I thought I had a chance. But I had no real idea how to initiate the conversation. This was my first proper assignment for a national news organisation. I needed five hundred words of nationalistic colour with a weepy patriot thrown in, but I couldn't approach a stranger and say, 'excuse me, sir, why are you blubbing like a toddler?'

In the end, I opted for subtlety (at least, I thought I was being subtle.) 'Hello, my name is Millie Lee, I'm a news reporter,' I said cheerily, flashing teeth and tapping my notepad. 'What do you think of the parade?'

'Damn good,' he said.

'Yes, it is, isn't it? Just what we needed after a tough few years.'

'Yah.' He waved a little Singapore flag in the air.

I said, 'When the armed forces came out just now, you seemed to get emotional.'

'Yah.'

'Why do you think you cried?'

He wiped his nose and glared at me. 'Eh? Where got crying?'

'Just now,' I insisted. 'I saw you wiping your eyes.'

'Allergy *lah*.'

'Oh, right. My photographer just took a picture of you. Thought you were emotional.'

'I am. Fed up with the dust. Too much dust in Singapore.'

'Yah.'

He pointed a condescending finger at me, the one typically used by older Chinese men to talk down to anyone younger or female. He said, 'You should do a story about dust in Singapore. Every day, I'm sniffing. My eyes are watering. It's no joke.'

'Right.' I checked my watch. I was getting desperate. 'Can I use your photo anyway?'

'What for?'

'It looks nice. You're waving your flag. Your eyes are filling up.'

'With dust! You gonna write about NDP dust is it?'

I laughed awkwardly, suddenly hating my job, my scholarship and my life choices in general. 'No, no, of course not.' I tapped my notepad again. I wasn't giving up. 'Can I ask you about the parade though?'

I was pleading, practically begging. I needed a usable quote, something, anything, that I could take back to Slick Scholar to demonstrate my potential. Technically, I didn't need permission to use the photo of Allergy Man. He was attending a public event at a public place. I didn't need to mention his emotional state – or his aversion to dusty surfaces – the juxtaposition would be enough. His weepy eyes. My prose. The readers would make the connection, subconsciously. And the sneaky juxtaposition might leave Mother Superior seriously pissed off.

So I pressed ahead. I said, 'Just a quick quote, maybe? How the parade has been for you. Can?'

I flashed my smile again. For two years, my braces had made me depressed every time I saw myself in the mirror of the school toilets. The braces made my dad angry every time he saw the bill. But they were worth it now.

My smile worked on people, particularly Chinese men and especially older Chinese men.

Allergy Man said, 'Yeah, OK.'

I could've kissed his snotty face. 'Great, thanks,' I said, flipping open the notepad. 'So what have you thought of the parade so far?'

'Too hot.'

My pen hovered above the notepad. 'Too hot?'

'Not enough shelter.'

'Understand, but what about the show itself?'

'Too long.'

I wanted to drop him into a silo filled with dust.

I said, 'Why did you come to the NDP?'

'My wife *lah*. Her company is involved this year. Made me paint my face some more.' He looked disgusted with himself.

I said, 'OK, well, thanks for your time. Can I just get your name?'

Allergy Man sat up straight. He put down his Singapore flag.

'Eh, why ah?'

'Why what?'

'Why you need my name?'

'Every quote I get must have a name to show that the quotes are real.'

'Better not.' He waved me away. I felt like a mosquito. 'My company might not like it.'

I said, 'You've only said the NDP is too long and too hot. You're not saying anything controversial.'

Allergy man shook his head and said, 'In Singapore, you never know. Cannot.'

I had never felt more patriotic.

As the uniformed staff of several Singaporean companies marched past the old City Hall building, I headed backstage and found myself with the Four Major Races. They were the co-hosts for the National Day Parade.

The Four Major Races were a bit like a United Nations cover band of Abba. There were two women and two men, but they were CMIO rather than Swedish. The Chinese-Malay-Indian-Others (CMIO) model is popular in Singapore, but essential at events like the NDP.

To mix things up, the Four Major Races included Chinese Personality, Malay Artiste, Indian Artiste and Eurasian Personality.

One day, I'll find out the difference between an artiste and a personality in Singapore. The Four Major Races were having their T-zones touched up and were rehearsing their next links.

Outside, brave pilots roared past in their patriotic phallic symbols. The top guns soared off towards the coastline – it didn't take long – which increased the tension backstage.

A sweaty, skinny guy hovered around the Four Major Races, speaking into a headset and nodding like a chicken attacking seeds. 'OK, OK, got it,' he shouted into the mic, before turning to the co-hosts. 'They say the energy is dropping outside,' he cried. 'This is what happens when you take sugary drinks out of their goodie bags.'

'It's no problem,' said Chinese Personality. He was the most handsome of the Four Major Races. He was also dressed in baggy shirt and pants like a hip-hop dancer. He was in his mid-forties.

'I'll say, "Sing-a-pore, let's make some noise",' he continued, far too enthusiastically for a grown man.

'You said that before the break,' said Indian artiste. 'I'll do my NDP rap.'

'No *lah*, no more rapping. They've got a rap in the main performance,' said Eurasian Personality. 'I'll just ask them if they're having a good time.'

'But the response might be muted,' said Headset Guy, looking increasingly perplexed.

'*Aiyah*, just do a quick call and response. Make them get louder and louder before we move on to the next segment,' said Malay Artiste.

'You've only got thirty seconds to do it,' said the melting Headset Guy.

'Can. No problem.'

The Four Major Races shared fist bumps and headed towards the main stage. This was my chance. Chinese Personality was at the back of the group and walking in my general direction. He was also the most famous of the quartet (obviously, he was Chinese).

'Excuse me, can I talk to you?' I touched his elbow.

He turned long enough to reveal the horror. To him, I wasn't a reporter. I was a groupie. I was an idiotic groupie grabbing at his idiotic hip-hop costume. 'Er, not really,' he said, trying to tear himself away.

As I lost my grip on his elbow, my hand slipped down his sweaty sleeve until it stopped at his palm, allowing my fingers to lock with his.

We were essentially holding hands. I was holding hands with a man who was expected to entertain a nation in approximating fifteen seconds. He was holding hands with a stalker.

I needed to explain my intentions better.

I said, 'I just need a quick one.'

That wasn't explaining my intentions better.

'No,' he insisted, trying to pull his hand from mine.

I needed to explain my intentions faster.

'I'll be done in a few seconds.'

Who was saying these words? Why were they coming from me?

'I'm going on stage now,' said Chinese Personality, literally removing my hand and placing it against my own thigh.

'OK, I'll be here when you get back.' I sounded pathetic.

He looked at me like I was a mangy stray about to be put down, and left. This time, there was a hand on my shoulder. Headset Guy threw me out of the backstage area.

So I didn't see the Four Major Races rally the crowd and work them into a noisy fervour before introducing hundreds of young dancers to the stage. I didn't see the dancers' hip-hop interpretation of this year's NDP theme – *Singapore, Always and*

Forever – alongside dozens of percussionists.

And I didn't see the star performer collapse on stage from nervous exhaustion or the medical crew whisk her away from camera phones as the NDP cut to a commercial. I didn't even hear the screams from the crowd.

Instead, I found myself in a darkened corridor with an empty notepad, wondering if it's possible to have a media scholarship cancelled in the first week. I heard a voice say, 'What are you writing about?'

I mumbled, 'Ah nothing, just scribbling.' I looked up. I had been joined by a pale teenager. She was sitting in a wheelchair, sipping water slowly. We were alone in the corridor.

'Are you OK?' I asked.

'Yeah. Just waiting for an ambulance.'

'What happened?'

'I fucked up the National Day Parade.'

I held her hand. I reassured her. I promised to keep her company until the ambulance arrived and then I hammered out a thousand words on a selfless young woman who had pushed her weary body to the limit in service of a grateful nation. Within minutes of filing the story, a giddy Slick Scholar called to inform me that he was pushing my hip-hop hero exclusive to the top of the home page. I floated out of the Padang and got drunk with Hokkien Half-Ball.

And then I had sex with Hokkien Half-Ball.

Day 5 – Morning

I stayed in bed and pretended to be asleep. This was difficult as Hokkien Half-Ball was singing *You'll Never Walk Alone* in the shower. I had to assume that he was either a Liverpool fan or had no sense of irony. I had walked alone in bed last night. The sex had not been great.

Being drunk hadn't helped, but the alcohol had also left Hokkien Half-Ball with flushed cheeks. It was like having sex with a tomato.

Fortunately, he didn't last long. He fell asleep on top of the thin sheet, still naked. It was a struggle to see him in the dark, especially through drunken eyes, but I won't be eating shrimp any time soon.

I felt him crawling across the bed. He said, 'How does it feel to have your first exclusive?'

Honestly, it felt great. I had wanted nothing else since I was a teenager, to see my name beneath a major headline, my byline, my words on a major news platform. I had waited years for this moment. I had dreamt of this moment. I just didn't want to share it with a naked lifestyle editor and his shrimp cocktail.

I thought about fake snoring. But I wasn't even sure if I snored in my sleep or how loudly. He might know now. He would know a lot of things about me now. And that made me angry, not for sleeping with him – we were both adults – but for being such a cliché. The ditzy new girl sleeps with the sleazy boss. I was starring in my own Korean drama. I was in no mood to look at him – or myself – right now. Besides, I was still hungover. I was feeling nauseous. I was genuinely worried that I might throw up if I rolled over and saw his manhood standing to attention. But I didn't want this moment sullied either. I had worked too hard for it, too many late nights studying, too many assignments, too many missed dinner dates to get the highest grades, to get the media scholarship and the chance for an exclusive like this.

I had to see my name above my words.

I rolled over. Thankfully, he was wearing a towel. He was picking at clumps of dried deodorant in his armpit hair. 'Oh, you're awake,' he said, grinning at me. Hokkien Half-Ball did have a cheeky smile.

'Yeah *lah*. Heard you singing in the shower just now,' I croaked, reaching for my phone on the bedside table, before stopping abruptly.

Was I naked beneath the sheets? I couldn't remember. I couldn't remember much, except for him insisting on paying for the hotel room in cash – which was classy – and him asking if I had any protection because the 7-Eleven was a long walk away – which was even classier.

My left hand felt a T-shirt and a pair of knickers. *Thank God.* I'd maintained a little dignity after the hazy euphoria had given way to mild self-loathing. Hokkien Half-Ball handed me his phone. 'Take a look,' he said, leaning across the crumpled bed. He had the faint outline of man-boobs. 'It's good.'

It really was. The layout exceeded my expectations. Huge headline. Prominent text. Decent photo of the dancer lying on a hospital bed. The page designers had even cobbled together a photo byline for me, lifting the goofy mugshot from my security pass.

I read the headline aloud.

'From hip-hop hero to hospital heartbreak.'

'Yeah, we love alliteration,' said Hokkien Half-Ball, flexing his pecs, presumably for my benefit, to show off his lean frame. But the man-boobs looked like they were blinking at me. 'So, how do you feel now?'

I sat up in bed. 'I feel good. First colour piece on my first major assignment. Wow. I've put the pressure on myself now.'

Hokkien Half-Ball looked crestfallen. 'No, I was talking about last night. Us. You know.'

'Oh that, yeah.' It was my turn to blush now. 'It was good. Yeah. Good.'

'I'm joking *lah*.'

'Bastard.' I threw a pillow at him.

'It was a fun night. Maybe do it again soon.' He threw the pillow back at me.

'Yeah, maybe,' I lied.

'Must get another exclusive first,' he said, giggling.

'Asshole,' I said, truthfully.

He stared at me for a bit. For several terrifying seconds I thought he was considering trying his luck again, one more for the road before heading back to the office to collect his bloody winnings from Peranakan Pervert.

The self-loathing was returning, in waves. I really didn't want to be here now. The thought of having sex with him a second time, sober and in the daylight, turned my stomach. I'd never touch seafood again.

He grinned at me. This was it. This was going to be my 'Me Too' moment, first week in the job, spurning the feeble advances of a randy supervisor in a cheap city hotel. But this wasn't sunny California. This was sweaty Singapore. Local women hadn't really had their 'Me Too' moment. I wasn't sure if we'd even had a moment yet. Hokkien Half-Ball was close enough for me to smell the Marlboro. He must have had one in the bathroom. He was practically marriage material.

'Come on *ah*,' he said. 'I've got more good news for you.'

I found myself gripping the bedsheet. 'Yeah? What's that?'

'The boss loves your story, thinks you've got a quirky writing style. Wants to meet you.'

I felt the tension dissipate. 'Really ah? Slick Scholar said that?'

'No, not that boss. *The* boss.'

Day 5 – Afternoon

In American movies, old-school media proprietors had framed news articles on their office walls. Captain Mayhem had a sepia-tinted photo of himself in the army. He also had that innate air of self-satisfaction that only comes with the finest education and people saluting you – and agreeing with you – for most of your adult life.

Captain Mayhem was always right because no one had ever accused him of being wrong.

Weirdly, he didn't look like a decorated soldier, but a *char siu bao*: pale, plump and wrinkled. He looked tiny in his high executive chair. His hair was aggressively parted from the side, presumably with a gardening rake.

Captain Mayhem hadn't been in the job long. Whenever the Singapore media industry needed a reinvention, they shook the banking and military trees until the coconuts dropped.

He had risen to the highest ranks of the Singapore army and was then rewarded with a prestigious seat on one of the world's largest banks. He was practically overqualified for a media job in Singapore.

He invited me to take a seat at his mahogany desk. There was a framed photograph of him in a suit and tie accepting something important from another Chinese man in a suit and tie.

'That was for a banking charity,' he said, reading my mind. 'My last job.'

'Oh right.'

I half-smiled, but I noticed his face drop. Had I sounded condescending? He waved a finger at me and said, 'You are cheeky.'

'What?'

He spun his laptop around. My National Day Parade piece was on the screen. He tapped my byline. 'You write cheeky pieces,' he said.

'Sorry,' I mumbled.

I was aware that I was turning red. That wasn't good. I kept seeing Hokkien Half-Ball looking down at me. I'm never eating tomatoes again.

Captain Mayhem said, 'You are a cheeky piece writer.'

Why wasn't he speaking properly? Was he having a stroke?

'I don't understand, Mr Mayhem.'

'Call me Captain.'

He winked at me. He actually winked at me. Why were male

journalists always winking at me in this place? Were they flirting or did they all have nervous twitches? I didn't call him by his first name. I would never call him by his first name. He said, 'We need more cheeky pieces like this. The first thing I did this morning was read your piece. And the second thing I did was call Slick Scholar. I told him. I want to meet this Millie Lee.'

'Thank you, sir.'

'Why you call me "sir"? Only my helper calls me "sir".'

'Sorry.'

He said, 'No, do not apologise. You are just what we need. My job here is to bring down our readership age. Young Singaporeans rarely read Singaporean news anymore. Why do you think that is?'

I had a vague idea. The reason was sitting across from me. Old generals and semi-retired bankers are rarely found at the cutting edge of digital media technology. Of course, I had a fallback answer. Young journalists always have a fallback answer to pacify old journalists looking to explain away their failings.

'Too many social media distractions,' I said.

'No, it's a lack of voices,' said Captain Mayhem.

Suddenly, I was intrigued. He was on the verge of sounding relevant here. 'What do you mean? I asked.

'Come on. You know. What's the real reason young people don't read local content?'

'Honestly?'

'Honestly.'

I took a breath. I had the most-read story in the country today. I was on a roll. Why not?

I said, 'Well, it's the perception of editorial interference and the self-censorship that has gone on for so many years. Even my NTU lecturers talked about it. And they used to work here. Readers don't trust us enough.'

'Not true,' cried Captain Mayhem. 'Every survey shows that Singaporeans trust our news reporting.'

'Who commissioned the surveys?'

'We did. But that's not the point. Our newsroom is full of respected, award-winning journalists?'

'Who gave them the awards?'

'We did. But that's not the point. Our in-house awards are well respected.'

'Where?'

'In-house.'

'Oh right.'

'And you could soon be among them.'

Captain Mayhem leaned across the desk. 'I'm thinking of nominating your cheeky piece for our feature story of the month. Considering you are such a young writer, it's one of the best pieces I've read in my media career.'

Captain Mayhem had been a media CEO for four months.

He tapped my photo byline and said, 'And I want more like that?'

'Young females?'

He roared with laughter. 'No. Well, yes. I want more cheeky pieces. Funny pieces. Human interest pieces. I've been saying to Slick Scholar. I watch short clips on TikTok almost every day. You know why or not? They're funny. We need more funny on our pages.'

Captain Mayhem stole a glimpse of my thighs as I crossed my

legs. 'We need more of you.'

I thanked him as I tugged at the edge of my skirt.

He said, 'No, thank you for this great piece. You are going to help us to reconnect with young Singaporeans. What do you know about monkeys?'

Day 5 – Evening

At the news conference, Hokkien Half-Ball brought in curry puffs for everyone. He made a point of thanking Peranakan Pervert for paying for them. Peranakan Pervert complained about the 'form guide' letting him down.

Slick Scholar had no clue what was going on but found their puerile bickering amusing. He asked if Peranakan Pervert had lost another bet.

'Of course he has,' said Mother Superior, not looking up from her demented scribbling. 'What did you expect?'

Then she peered over the top of her glasses, towards me. She didn't speak at first. I felt exposed. I was sure she was going to jab a finger in my face and call me a whore.

Instead, she said, 'Your story today, not bad. Quite quirky.' I expressed my sincere thanks, out of relief more than anything else. 'But cannot edit,' said Mother Superior. She looked at the giggling, leering men sitting among us and then said, 'But I suppose that doesn't matter, right?'

'What does that mean?' I was surprised at my aggressive tone.

'It doesn't mean anything,' said Slick Scholar quickly. 'Tell us about your monkey story.'

It wasn't my monkey story. It was Captain Mayhem's monkey story. 'I'm going to speak to the Mandai people later,' I muttered.

'Great,' said Slick Scholar, clapping his hands together. 'Right, let's move on. I've had a request to make the new minister more relatable. So let's do a photo shoot with him at a hawker centre.'

Day 6 – Morning

I had a dream about Mother Superior last night. We were in the Bukit Timah rainforest together. But she was wearing a monkey costume, jabbing her red pen at me and singing, *I Wanna Be Like You.*

And then Hokkien Half-Ball chased us through the forest.

Day 6 – Evening

I spent several sweaty hours with several sweaty spokespeople of the Singapore Wildlife Sanctuary Group. They were devoted to preserving Singapore's wildlife, as long as their sanctuary group made money.

We met at a quiet road near the Central Catchment Nature Reserve, which was home to more than five hundred native animal species. And the Singapore Wildlife Sanctuary Group was doing its best to kill all of them.

Not officially, of course.

Officially, the spokespeople insisted that the Singapore Wildlife Sanctuary Group was *enhancing* the island's biggest green lung – by chopping chunks of it down. A hub of wildlife parks is going to be built to replace the displaced wildlife. This makes total sense to a country that knocks down a rainforest to build a condo called Rainforest Residences. It just doesn't make much sense to the indigenous fauna. One minute, a monkey is hanging out among the trees. The next, it's hanging off the side of a taxi, which made for a viral video on TikTok last week. But the video clip created a real problem for the PR department at the Singapore Wildlife Sanctuary Group. The monkeys were still being spotted around the unfinished eco-tourism hub, eating fruit and looking really cute.

They were also being spotted on the roads around the eco-tourism hub, looking really dead.

This is not good for Singapore. Why? Because this is a billion-dollar investment. This is not good for Captain Mayhem. Why? Because he sits on the board of the billion-dollar investment.

And this is not good for me. Why? Because I'm expected to find a positive, uplifting story about long-tailed macaques that doesn't involve roadkill.

I was expected to coax this feel-good feature from the corporate communications department. The Singapore Wildlife Sanctuary Group's PR staff were all dressed like a conservative version of Dora the Explorer and Bruce Wayne's butler, half intrepid explorer, half corporate lackey. And they all had iPads, constantly checking their pre-approved soundbites and nodding at everything I said, in unison, like a chorus line of puppies.

And they all spoke robotically.

'Since we built rope bridges for the long-tailed macaques, there has been a seventy-eight per cent increase in safe passages from one side of the road to the other,' said the director of the corporate communications division, sustainability and conservation, Singapore Wildlife Sanctuary Group.

That was his complete title. I won't type it out in full again. I have a life.

'Yes, seventy-eight per cent,' echoed the deputy director.

'I have all the figures in this file,' said another young executive, handing me a six-page press release I'd already read online. The press release came in a card folder, along with a calendar, a diary and a plastic flask in a reusable bag, on behalf of the sustainability and conservation division.

'Yes, thank you,' I said, reluctantly accepting the tote bag. I was already carrying a rucksack and holding my phone and notepad. 'I read the figures in the press release.'

I followed the trio along a boardwalk, which was built after developers cleared the outer forest to offer tourists a clearer view of the inner forest.

The director said, 'We've also built camera traps to monitor the monkeys across our different eco-corridors. We've counted six hundred and fifty-eight safe passages.'

The deputy director said, 'Yes, six hundred and fifty-eight safe passages.'

The young executive said, 'Yes, the figures are all in the press release.'

'Yes, I read them last night,' I said. 'I also read about the resort you're building in an area that wildlife groups said was home to our most endangered animals.'

The director stopped to wipe his forehead. 'Absolutely. Our sustainable solutions department are overseeing that one, using recycled materials. It's going to be called Animal Paradise.'

The deputy director said, 'Yes, Animal Paradise. All recycled materials.'

The young executive said, 'Yes, the details are all in the press release.'

I said, 'But seven pangolins were found dead near the proposed site of Animal Paradise.'

'Yeah, we might have to rethink the name,' said the director.

His raised eyebrow didn't seem particularly keen on my line of enquiry. Or maybe it was the Botox. His face looked like it hadn't moved since 2012. I'm always fascinated by men of my father's generation, retaining their jet-black hair and removing the crow's feet to preserve the essence of youth. Most looked like a stretched scrotum.

I held up my notepad to the trio and said, 'Do you have any idea why the roadkill numbers are still so high for the long-tailed macaques, despite your safety measures?'

The director smiled at me, patronisingly, like I was a toddler offering him a toy. 'I think that might be above my pay grade,' he said, chuckling.

'It's certainly above my pay grade,' said the deputy director.

Their laughter echoed through the patchy forest.

'Then it's definitely above mine,' said the young executive.

At this point, they looked like they might wet themselves.

The director stopped laughing and said, 'Speaking of pay grades, how's my old *kaki*, Captain Mayhem?'

'Yeah, he's good,' I spluttered, getting the message.

'We went to the same school, you know,' he added, making sure I really got the message.

'I didn't know that.'

Though I should've guessed.

'Anyway, let's continue the tour,' the director boomed, his false jollity restored. 'You must see what Animal Paradise is going to look like.'

'Yes, it'll be made entirely from recycled materials,' said the deputy director.

'Yes, the details are in the press release,' said the executive.

'Yeah, I read them last night,' I mumbled in submission.

Day 7 – Morning

My feature on the delicate balancing act between wildlife protection and economic growth was cut to six paragraphs.

The headline read, 'Singapore prepares for Animal Paradise'.

Day 7 – Evening

Captain Mayhem sent me the following email after work:

Hey Millie,

Great job on the Wildlife Sanctuary piece. The

director loved it too. He wanted to buy you dinner sometime to thank you.

You're so popular!

Captain Mayhem

I deleted the email and polished off the wine in my Singapore Wildlife Sanctuary Group reusable cup.

Day 8

Uncle Groper handed me my first hate mails, which made me want to gag. Uncle Groper had been fiddling with his testicles on the walk over.

'For you *lah*,' he said, passing me two pieces of A4.

'Why did you print this, uncle?'

'The desk likes to keep a record.'

That wasn't true. Uncle Groper liked to keep a record. He had been a sub-editor on the desk since Lee Kuan Yew was prime minister. He was very fond of telling us that Lee Kuan Yew had once walked past his cubicle and smiled at him. Uncle Groper was the last of the old-school sub-editors. He didn't understand web design, social media or search engine optimisation. Apparently, Hokkien Half-Ball had once asked Uncle Groper for his views on SEO and the *ah pek* said he only liked '*Mr Blue Sky*'.

I didn't get the joke either.

At least I went online to find out about Electric Light Orchestra (ELO). Uncle Groper still didn't know what SEO was.

(He was right about '*Mr Blue Sky*' though. It is a great song.)

Uncle Groper just did text subbing. He never missed a comma or a chance for a bad sex pun in a lifestyle headline.

Uncle Groper didn't lay out web pages and hadn't written a story since I was in diapers.

Uncle Groper earned three times my salary.

I think he was paid by the comma.

So he took it upon himself to print and compile readers' feedback, even though most of the feedback came from readers who had the time and temperament to sit down and write such feedback.

Plato said never give power to those who crave it. Uncle Groper gave too much credence to lunatics. He trusted their judgement. I wouldn't trust them with soft toilet paper.

I held the hate mails at arm's length as if they were explosive devices.

Uncle Groper said, 'Just read them *lah*. Cannot ignore them. Even Auntie Soh from Sembawang has a right to an opinion.'

Every journalist in Singapore must have hated Auntie Soh from Sembawang at some stage of their media careers.

Auntie Soh from Sembawang was Uncle Groper's go-to fictional creation to make a point. He loved to bring her up during his story dissections.

Is Auntie Soh from Sembawang going to understand your intro?

Can Auntie Soh from Sembawang follow your tech jargon?

Will Auntie Soh from Sembawang get your *cheem* English?

Does Auntie Soh from Sembawang have the patience to read so many quotes?

I didn't know Auntie Soh from Sembawang. But she sounded really fucking stupid. Still, Uncle Groper insisted that every reader had a right to his or her opinion. And journalists had to respect such opinions.

I appreciated the libertarian sentiment, but it was hard to take Uncle Groper seriously when he was scratching his balls at the same time.

But I did as I was told. I read my first hate mail:

To Millie Lee,

I read your one-sided story about the Singapore Wildlife Sanctuary Group. We are a small nation. We do not have the luxury of space, like other countries. We must feed our families first, not a few monkeys in the forest. I think you are very young. I think you do not understand how the Singapore economy works. We need tourist dollars. Please be more balanced in your reporting next time.

Then I read my second email:

To Millie Lee,

I didn't expect much from your one-sided article when I read the headline. Singapore prepares for Animal Paradise. Is that a joke? Since the development began, the forest has been decimated and roadkill incidents have clearly risen. We can build hotels any time. We cannot build new forests. Might I suggest that you do more reading about the devastation of our biodiversity before paying lip service to the latest cash grab. Your piece was naïve and dangerous. Your job is to be objective, not help greedy corporations. They are already destroying the planet. Why are you helping them?

After the evening conference, I shared both letters with Slick Scholar.

The national editor said, 'Yeah, it's great. More than five hundred comments on Facebook so far. Must go back and do a follow-up at some point. We need a personal story next.'

'From a monkey?'

'Absolutely.' He winked at me and headed upstairs for a debrief with Captain Mayhem.

Over drinks later, Lauren pointed out that the Singapore Wildlife Sanctuary Group had placed a couple of banner ads on our homepage.

So it was good to know that my work hadn't been entirely wasted.

Day 15

Peranakan Pervert, Hokkien Half-Ball and Uncle Groper were gathered around a computer terminal.

'Too small *lah*,' said Hokkien Half-Ball.

'No *lah*, just nice,' insisted Peranakan Pervert.

'At *my* age, any size can already,' said Uncle Groper.

They laughed far too loudly, stopping only when Peranakan Pervert caught me walking in their general direction.

'Ah, Millie, come.' He waved me over. 'Come and see this.'

Uncle Groper hurried to move his plastic soup container to one side. He pushed his cigarettes from his keyboard. I always found his chivalrous efforts to tidy his desk for a young woman strangely touching. It made a nice change from touching himself. He ushered me towards his desk. But as he was sitting and I was standing, his eyeline found my breasts and his hand found the edge of my left butt-cheek. I brushed it off, in every sense. Uncle Groper was a product of his generation. He reminded me of my elderly uncle, on my mother's side, who sulked for a week when Yangtze Theatre shut down. They were not sinister, really, just sleazy *ah peks*. Every culture has its sleazy *ah peks*. And in our office, Uncle Groper was the last dirty old man standing.

He was almost dribbling.

I could see why. A young, slender Chinese woman was sunbathing on the screen. The scene looked incongruous. Something was odd.

Finally, I pointed at the screen and said, 'Isn't that …?'

'Yep,' giggled Peranakan Pervert.

'But that's outside a …'

'Yep,' chuckled Hokkien Half-Ball.

'Cannot, right?'

'Not sure. We want you to go and find out,' said Peranakan Pervert.

'Why? What's the story?'

'It's had a million views on TikTok. That's the story,' said Hokkien Half-Ball.

The interest was obvious. An attractive woman, barely out of her teens, was lying on a sun lounger, in a bikini, next to a void-deck, in full view of a housing estate. The three men couldn't tear themselves away. I was beginning to think most of the million views came from them.

I asked what they wanted me to cover.

'Cover them.' Uncle Groper tittered like a schoolboy at his double entendre.

'Cover what?' I said. 'Her breasts? I think they're covered.'

'Barely. Anyway, just go down and interview her,' said Hokkien Half-Ball. 'Could be a good talking point for the lifestyle section?'

I tightened my ponytail, struggling to stay calm. 'But what's the story? Is she breaking any HDB rules? She's just sunbathing, right?'

'Maybe check out the laws on public decency,' said Peranakan Pervert.

'She's not naked,' I said. 'There's nothing indecent here.'

'That's true,' agreed Uncle Groper.

The old man's legs jiggled beneath his desk. I suspect he missed Yangtze Theatre too.

'Some are saying she's sending the wrong message to young people,' said Hokkien Half-Ball, the newsroom's new spokesperson on morality.

I said, 'She's sending the wrong message on skin cancer. That's about it.' Peranakan Pervert sighed and placed a patronising hand on my shoulder. 'Millie, try and take emotion out of it. This is unusual behaviour in Singapore. This is a news story. Go and find the girl and get her side. If she feels she's done nothing wrong, fine, but give her a chance to share her story. Then get a couple of quotes from neighbours and HDB and you've covered all angles.

Can?'

'Yeah, OK,' I muttered. 'But it's not going to be sensationalist, is it?'

'Of course not.'

Peranakan Pervert was now lightly massaging my shoulder.

Uncle Groper's knees were thumping the underside of his desk.

Hokkien Half-Ball's gaze was switching between the computer screen and my chest. He was making comparisons.

Suddenly, the prospect of discussing a young woman's tanning technique appealed. I just wanted to get out of the office. I agreed to do the piece, not that I had much choice.

I was still on probation.

But I told them that I wasn't keen on writing anything exploitative.

'Of course not,' said Peranakan Pervert. 'But she must wear the bikini for the photo shoot.'

Day 17

I made the mistake of speaking to residents first. Bedok is a curious mix of East Coast rich and heartland poor and the sunbather had divided opinion. I started with an elderly Chinese couple, coming back from the wet market. They seemed jovial and friendly. They were surprisingly talkative, in a mixture of Mandarin, English and Singlish.

The husband said, 'People should mind their business.'

'You never mind your business,' the wife interjected. 'You kept looking at the *China girl* photo in the Chinese papers.'

'Need to see which block she stay at.'

His wife asked why.

'So me and friends can hang out at her void deck.'

He laughed until his wife hit him with her *bok choy*.

I was intrigued by the woman's comment on nationality and wondered why she thought the sunbather was from China.

She rolled her eyes and said, 'Please *lah*. Trying to get a Singapore husband.'

'No need to try very hard,' her husband chuckled.

She hit him with the *bok choy* again.

An hour later, I tracked down the woman who had initially reported the sunbather to our online media team. She even invited me into her home.

Her HDB flat was neat, but sparse, with traditional furniture and a shrine along the far wall. She was stick thin and kept tugging at a cardigan, even though the non-air-conditioned flat was stifling.

I asked her how she'd managed to capture the woman in action. 'Not the first time,' she said, clutching at her cardigan. 'I walked past her last time. Didn't say anything. I ran up here and tried to take a photo, but she'd gone already. So I waited by the window to catch her sunbathing.'

I was astonished. 'You did this every day?'

'No *lah*. Not when it was raining.'

That made sense.

I asked why she objected to the young woman sunbathing,

considering she hadn't broken any HDB rules.

Cardigan Woman said, 'Too much of this now in Singapore.'

'Too much of what?'

She sat up straight and said, 'Western lifestyle.'

I asked if sunbathing was a western lifestyle.

Cardigan Woman said, 'It's everything now with these women. Show off too much.' She gestured towards my sleeveless top. 'It's dangerous. There is a primary school nearby.'

I looked up from my notepad. 'Why is sunbathing dangerous for primary school children? The UV rays?'

She pursed her lips. 'You're young. But we never used to do this in Singapore. And now, everything can, since 377A.'

She pulled the cardigan across her chest and turned away from me in disgust. She recoiled at the mention of 377A.

My curiosity got the better of me. 'How do you think the 377A law repeal on homosexuality relates to this woman sunbathing?'

Cardigan Woman said, 'We are an Asian society. We don't want this near primary schools.'

'Sunbathers or gay men?'

'*Both.*'

I left thinking only of sunbathing gay men.

By sunset, I had covered two hawker centres, the wet market, the sports complex and even popped into Bedok Mall in a shallow attempt to find younger people around McDonald's.

The teenagers didn't care about the sunbather.

Young women were either indifferent or mildly hostile.

Young men were either indifferent or mildly aroused.

Old women mostly loathed the sunbather's arrogance and

one old man asked if I could WhatsApp the photos across to his battered iPhone.

When I pointed out that his ancient phone wasn't equipped to receive such heavy data, he asked if he could take a photo of my breasts instead.

Actually, he asked to take a photo of me but pointed at my boobs. I declined his request.

As I headed towards the Bedok MRT station, I caught him taking photos of me anyway.

Maybe he was an ass man.

At 8pm, I filed my copy with as much balance as I could muster, considering it was a non-story about a non-event.

At 8.15pm, Mother Superior removed the quotes and all references to the 377A law repeal as they were not relevant. The sunbather was not a man. Or gay. Or biologically capable of homosexual intercourse with another man. I thanked her for pointing all this out to me. I hadn't been sure.

At 9pm, Hokkien Half-Ball cleared the story and instructed Uncle Groper to come up with a pithy headline for my feature.

At 9.15pm, Uncle Groper came up with the headline, 'Women's chest tips neighbours over edge'.

At 9.30pm, Mother Superior savaged Uncle Groper's headline for its puerile juxtaposition. She really hated juxtaposition. She didn't seem to like chest tips much either.

At 10pm, Slick Scholar changed the headline to, 'Sunbather leaves Bedok residents browned off'.

At 10.05pm, I wandered over to Uncle Groper's cubicle and said, 'I don't get the headline.'

'Browned off is a bit archaic *lah*,' he said. 'It means fed-up, like pissed off. It's very British. Our editor was educated at Cambridge *wha'*.'

At 10.30pm, Captain Mayhem called down and demanded to know why the sunbather's headline made no sense. Why were Bedok residents browned off? Were they being cooked?

Captain Mayhem was not educated at Cambridge.

At 10.45pm, Slick Scholar offered 'Sunbather burns Bedok residents'.

At 10.50pm, Uncle Groper wandered over to my cubicle. 'I don't get the headline,' he whispered.

So I said, 'Young people use burn as a putdown. A burn is a putdown. But it's being used wrongly here.'

At 11pm, my story went online with the following headline: 'Scantily clad sunbathing woman polarises Bedok neighbours'.

She wasn't scantily clad. But according to the digital media team, 'scantily clad sunbathing woman' might do well in porn searches.

Day 18

I woke up with a sense of unease. Without looking at my phone, I suspected that I'd written the most popular story in the country again. The messages soon confirmed it. Scantily Clad Sunbathing Woman had given me more page hits, shares and retweets than any other journalist in Singapore.

Going viral with clickbait made me think about my teenage aspirations. When I was a Mass Comm student at NTU, our associate professor specialised in film studies and made us watch several media-related movies to inspire his idealistic herd.

The first movie was *All the President's Men*, which had great haircuts and a far-fetched storyline. Two men brought down a government. How was this going to happen in Singapore? Mother Superior would've trashed Bernstein and Woodward's copy for not following the official press release.

The second movie was *The Insider*, which was about a whistleblower bringing down big business. He might as well have been a pixie bringing down a big toadstool. Do we have whistleblowers in Singapore? I'm not sure if we're even allowed to have whistles.

And the third movie was *Spotlight*, which resonated with me because it was about journalists investigating child sex abuse in the Roman Catholic Church. When I was in junior college, I asked if I could study the movie as part of my interdisciplinary programme research on the media's impact on society.

My teacher said the subject was off-limits and irrelevant. I pointed out that the case involved the Catholic Church and I attended a Catholic school. So it was quite relevant.

I added that the interdisciplinary programme expected me to go beyond the syllabus, to think outside of the box and challenge conventional wisdom. As a journalist, would I not be expected to ask awkward questions about difficult subjects? My teacher sent me to the principal for being awkward and difficult.

But I loved *Spotlight*. I was still a teenager when I first watched the movie and naively clung to the idea of being paid to write stuff that changed the world for the better.

I knew the reality was always going to be different. I was

idealistic, not stupid. I just didn't expect to produce articles that invited debate about the perfect breast size.

Apparently, the pair belonging to Scantily Clad Sunbathing Woman were not big enough to warrant so much attention, according to the anonymous posts in our comments section.

Luckily, a guy had kindly pasted a link to a site that included women with 'real tits'.

His post had almost as many likes as my story.

As I returned to Bedok for the inevitable follow-up story, I received a WhatsApp message from Hokkien Half-Ball.

> *'Uncle Groper just got reprimanded again. An intern caught him looking at a website called Real Tits.'*

I can't see anyone making a movie about my journalism career.

In the afternoon, I made a breakthrough in the story that interested everyone except me. After a bit of a wild goose chase and neighbours sending me to the wrong block, floor and unit, I finally found the HDB flat of Scantily Clad Sunbathing Woman. I knocked several times but there was no answer. I was about to leave when I caught a silhouette running from one room to another. Even though the tinted windows were closed and the grilles locked, it was clearly a slim woman.

It was her.

I tried my luck again, tapping the window this time.

I said, 'Er, hello, it's Millie Lee. I'm a reporter. Can I talk to you, please?'

The silhouette suddenly appeared on the other side of the tinted window. If I'm being honest, she made me jump back slightly.

I asked again if I could to speak to her.

She said, 'You're the one who wrote a story about me.'

Her voice barely made it through the glass.

'Yeah, I did,' I said, maybe a bit too cheerily.

'Fuck you,' she said.

I deserved that.

I was already on my way back to the lift when I heard the window being dragged open.

She poked her head through the gap. She was crying.

Day 20

I spent most of the day and half the night with the woman. She lived with her parents, but they never came out once to speak to me. They locked their bedroom door and stayed there. I had to talk over their Korean dramas for hours until they eventually fell asleep.

The woman clearly hated me – and understandably so – but didn't really want me to leave either. She had no one else to talk to. She kept dabbing her eyes, tugging at a box of tissues on the IKEA coffee table, but it didn't make much difference. She wept through most of our chat.

'They keep calling me a slut,' she said. 'You know that?'

I didn't know that. But I didn't need to know that either. I knew she was telling the truth. One of the first rules of rookie reporting: never read the comments. They're often vile.

In Singapore, we need a permit to speak at Speakers' Corner. So, we store it. Churn it. And then spit it out all over social media. Anonymously, of course.

She said, 'I'm not a slut, OK?'

'I know,' I whispered.

'How you know? You don't know me.'

'No, I don't. Tell me about yourself.'

I shuddered. The words sounded shit, even in my head.

She snarled at me and said, 'Why? So you get another big story, is it?'

I left the question hanging, probably because neither of us liked the obvious answer. Of course, I wanted another viral story. I wanted another byline. I wanted more likes, shares and retweets. I was another shallow product of my TikTok generation. And I was self-aware enough to know it, too, which made it even worse. I knew exactly what I was doing.

I told her that it was important that she shared her side of the story.

She said, 'What story? I was just sunbathing outside my house.' I didn't notice any tan lines. She was wearing a long-sleeved shirt and leggings, consciously covering all the fleshy parts that my story had exposed to a grateful nation.

'You live quite near to the Bedok park,' I mumbled.

'Yah? So? I had too much poly homework. No time. I just wanted a break from them,' she said, nodding towards her parents' bedroom door.

I said, 'Too much stress about your schoolwork?'

'Too much arguing.'

And then she told me that her boyfriend had dumped her over WhatsApp. His poly friends were making fun of him in class. The poly had also asked her to study at home for a few days. Her mother had told her to do the same because the neighbours were gossiping.

And her father had refused to be in the same room with her. His coffee shop friends had made fun of his daughter's photo.

So he'd retaliated by calling her a slut.

She asked me not to publish another story. She begged me to leave her alone.

At 6pm, I was invited to the evening conference to explain my reasons for not wanting to write another story about Scantily Clad Sunbathing Woman. The piece was still tracking well on all digital platforms. There were rumours that the issue might be addressed in Parliament. We didn't have earthquakes or military invasions for MPs to discuss.

We just had Scantily Clad Sunbathing Woman.

Peranakan Pervert was particularly disappointed. He was my direct supervisor. I was still on probation. I hadn't openly defied him before. I hadn't slept with him either. His painful flirting felt a bit like being attacked by mosquitoes at MacRitchie. No matter how many times I waved them away, the cheeky comments kept on coming. I understood his pressure. Peranakan Pervert was an older man. He was maybe twenty-five years older than both Hokkien Half-Ball and Slick Scholar. Hokkien Half-Ball already had more responsibility, overseeing two different desks. Slick Scholar was on a fast track to parliament, as long as he avoided public scandal and regurgitated the press releases in a timely fashion.

But Peranakan Pervert's career was drifting. And Captain Mayhem had been appointed to remove the last of the deadwood in the building. Peranakan Pervert needed an interview with Scantily Clad Sunbathing Woman much more than I did.

'This story still has legs,' he insisted.

'So does she,' muttered Hokkien Half-Ball.

Peranakan Pervert didn't laugh this time. He loved schoolboy humour, but not as much as he loved a fixed salary with regular CPF contributions.

At the head of the long mahogany table, Slick Scholar stared at me, as if I were the only person in the room.

His tight, angular jaw came from those daily runs, chin-ups and burpees (he often posted his workouts on Instagram).

His confidence came from the kind of company he kept on those workouts (business leaders and members of parliament).

And his knowledge came from the school where he met those business leaders and members of parliament (one of the best in Singapore, all boys, all-knowing, all-powerful).

He said, 'Millie, what are your reservations about this story?'

God, his voice was smooth. He had that educated local accent. He was clearly Singaporean, but his accent was comfortably understood at conferences everywhere.

I repeated the promise I'd made to her, not to write another story. Slick Scholar said, 'Completely understand. But if we did that every time we were asked, we'd have nothing to write except government press releases.' The joke was almost too obvious. But everyone in the room sensibly let it pass.

I said, 'People are calling her a slut, even her own father. Plus, her boyfriend dumped her as soon as the story came out.'

I saw their backs straighten. I was digging a deeper hole for myself.

'You're making the story sound even better,' said Hokkien Half-Ball.

'You have to do it,' added Peranakan Pervert, rather desperately.

'I'm inclined to agree,' said Slick Scholar. 'Keep it balanced. Add your usual nuance. Give both sides. See if you can speak to the boyfriend.'

'Why should he get any publicity?' I asked, far too loudly. 'He's an asshole.'

'Language,' muttered Mother Superior, who once made an intern burst into tears by calling him a 'fucking idiot'.

Slick Scholar said, 'OK, leave out the boyfriend. Just write it sensitively and I'll help you afterwards. I'll clear the copy. OK?'

Our national editor got up to leave. The evening conference was over. He had ordered me to do something that I clearly did not want to do. And yet, somehow, I was supposed to feel gratitude for his kind offer of help.

On my way out, Peranakan Pervert thanked me for agreeing to write the follow-up. I hadn't.

He promised to handle the story sensitively and then he handled me sensitively by patting me on the back, his fingertips just catching the edge of my left breast.

Day 21

I convinced Scantily Clad Sunbathing Woman to do an interview. I convinced her that her side of the story would stop all the online speculation. I convinced her that talking to me was in her best interest.

She believed me, which was astonishing.

I didn't believe myself.

After the interview, I returned home and took a long shower, but it made no difference.

I still felt unclean.

Day 22

My day off was going to be spent with Lauren. We were going for coffee and clothes shopping in Orchard.

But my day off was ruined when I read the published version of my Scantily Clad Sunbathing Woman interview.

First, she was still scantily clad in description, presumably the work of Uncle Groper. Second, the asshole-boyfriend-dumping incident had been added to the piece, presumably the work of Peranakan Pervert.

And third, the asshole boyfriend had been contacted for that all-important 'balance'. I later discovered that he'd been contacted by a harassed intern, who studied at the same polytechnic and had been ordered by Hokkien Half-Ball to make the most of her poly contacts.

On the plus side, most of the negative comments were now being directed towards the ex-boyfriend.

And then my phone rang.

'I've had to file a police report,' said a raging male voice. 'I've had my IC details and my home address posted online. Everyone is abusing me and my family, thanks to you. Bitch.'

At least I had found that all-important balance.

Both parties hated me equally now.

Day 22

A government minister shared her views on Scantily Clad Sunbathing Woman this evening, pointing out that 'the media had a responsibility to be balanced and avoid sensationalist coverage in the chase for eyeballs'.

She was speaking on the sidelines of a climate change conference. Her views on Scantily Clad Sunbathing Woman became the most-read story in our Singapore section.

Her speech on climate change didn't make the top ten.

Day 25

A local airline company ran a guerrilla advertising campaign for budget flights on our news website today.

The ad read: 'Cannot sunbathe at an HDB? Get your tan in Bali.'

Scantily Clad Sunbathing Woman went viral for a third time. I called her to apologise. Her phone line had been disconnected.

Day 30

Slick Scholar called me into his office today. He wanted to commend me for my variety of stories in my first month and insisted that he owed me *makan* for doing the interview with the sunbathing woman. Apparently, my work had been noticed. Captain Mayhem was keen to make further changes to the newsroom and my name had been mentioned as a future features writer and columnist in the lifestyle section.

'Isn't that Lauren's job?' I wondered.

'At the moment,' said Slick Scholar. 'She's eager to move forward. I need young voices across the desk, young female voices especially, if we're going to survive in the long-term.'

At dinner, I told my parents that my bosses were impressed with my work so far. My father pointed out that there was no money or prestige in working for the Singapore media anymore, unlike last time.

My mother was more supportive. She always read the lifestyle sections in the Chinese media and asked when I'd be interviewing Channel 8 actors. She was obviously proud. She gave me an extra, heaped spoonful of rice and then reminded me that lifestyle journalists cannot be fat.

Day 35

At 7am this morning, I found myself back in school, reciting the National Pledge. I stood with a thousand sleepy students. I faced the Singapore flag and pledged to build a democratic society based on justice and equality.

After that, I discreetly pulled out my phone and re-watched a school video that compared gay men to monkeys.

The video had gone viral yesterday, which was more than enough for the news editors to dispatch me for the obvious follow-up. The footage was a bit grainy and shaky, because a student had sneakily filmed a counsellor's presentation on sex education. The counsellor's first slide was entitled 'STRAIGHT TALK' with a cartoonish depiction of a man and a woman holding hands. Subtle.

Then he reeled off several statistics.

According to his slideshow, fifty per cent of gay men lived with gonorrhoea.

According to his slideshow, more than seventy-five per cent of gay men believed that sex with children was acceptable.

And, according to his slideshow, a small percentage of gay men had no issue with bestiality.

His slideshow presentation was for secondary school boys.

His standout slide, though, was a photograph of an emaciated monkey, accompanied with his observation that AIDS had originated from this particular breed of monkey.

He asked his terrified audience to think about how AIDS

might have spread from the emaciated monkey to mankind. Again, subtle.

As he wrapped up, the counsellor seemed to suggest that homosexuals were somehow complicit in the spread of Covid-19, but he was a little vague on the details.

Perhaps a Wuhan resident had enjoyed gay sex with a bat.

His sex talk concluded with no useful talk about sex whatsoever, just a final slide of that emaciated monkey beneath the headline: 'AIDS!'

I put away my phone and thought about those terrified boys in the audience. They'd never visit the Singapore Zoo again.

After the school assembly, I was ushered into the principal's office. The walls were decorated with slogans and motivational quotes about being the best, becoming the best or being the best for others.

Singaporean schools are smothered in mottos. It's not a bad thing. I just wished they paid as much attention to homophobic PowerPoint presentations as they did to inspirational décor.

The principal sat back in his chair and clasped his hands together. For a second, I thought he was going to ask me to join him in prayer. But he hummed a lot instead. 'Hmm, the incident was very unfortunate,' he said. 'But the materials were not approved by anyone at school. The counsellor acted independently.'

I asked what the vetting process was like when it came to sex education.

The principal said, 'Hmm, yes. They will all be vetted in future.'

I said, 'What kind of counselling will be offered?'

‘That’s really up to him.’

‘I meant for the students.’

‘Oh, right. Hmm. Yes.’

I delicately reminded the principal that his students had seen slides linking homosexuality to bestiality.

The principal winced at the mention of *homosexuality*. ‘Hmm, yes, of course. Every student will be offered counselling as soon as we bring one in.’

I was shocked. ‘You don’t have a counsellor?’

‘We did,’ said the principal. ‘He gave the sex education talk.’

In the evening, Uncle Groper discreetly called me over to his cubicle. I feared the worst. I had written a story on sex education. Uncle Groper bookmarked porn sites. This was not going to end well.

He pulled out the chair beside him and said, ‘Come. Sit *lah*.’

I straightened my skirt and sat at a slight angle away from him. Years on the MRT had made these movements instinctive.

‘Your story. Too emotional,’ he whispered.

I was immediately on the defensive. Uncle Groper had never questioned the *tone* of my writing before. That wasn’t his job. He was a sub-editor, an old-fashioned check sub, the final gatekeeper before the story was published online. Nothing got past him. He was forensic in his checking. Never missed a comma or a grammatical error. But it wasn’t his place to challenge the *feel* of a piece. It wasn’t even the time for him to do it.

My story hadn’t gone through the editing process, the usual hierarchy. Ordinarily, Peranakan Pervert settled the angle of the piece. Mother Superior did the initial demolishing. I did the rebuilding and then the story moved along to a sub-editor – and possibly Slick Scholar if the story was going to be prominently placed – before finally ending up in Uncle Groper's basket.

But he had picked up my untouched, raw copy.

I told him that the story hadn't been edited yet.

He said, 'I know *lah*. But I was curious. So I take a look first. Your writing is too judgemental. Look.' He scrolled through the text. 'You've deliberately picked out quotes that make the principal look homophobic. Look at this one *ah*. Blur like *sotong*.'

'It's what he said,' I shrugged.

'I know. But what is Mother Superior's obsession?'

I sighed. 'Juxtaposition.'

'Correct. And the principal's quote there, next to your paragraph, makes the school sound intolerant and homophobic, when it's probably just an innocent mistake. These schools have hundreds of trainers and outside instructors. Hard to keep track.'

I had never seen the old man so invested in a story before. I said, 'I'm just reporting what the principal said.'

Uncle Groper said, 'No *lah*, you're *judging*. And you're giving your reader a chance to judge *you*. The more you push your agenda—'

'I'm not pushing an agenda,' I interrupted.

Uncle Groper raised a hand to patiently silence me. He said, 'The more you push your agenda, the more they will push back. You're young *lah*. You think you are helping. But no one likes to be pushed. Don't give them a chance to push back.' He delicately tapped my hand, but not in *that* way. Nothing like that way. And I understood. The porn sites. The bookmarks. The exaggerated innuendos. It was obvious now, hiding in plain sight.

So I rewrote my story for Uncle Groper with no editorialising flourishes. Just the facts.

Even Mother Superior was impressed. 'Not bad,' she said, very begrudgingly, as she sent my edited copy away. 'When I saw your name down for this story, I expected another one of your grandstanding pieces, like the NDP one. But this was solid.'

Captain Mayhem was equally pleased. He even sent me an email, expressing his admiration for my handling of such a delicate social issue.

Captain Mayhem and the school principal were members of the same country club.

Day 38

Peranakan Pervert sent me to a bus stop today. But this was no ordinary bus stop. This was a bus stop with a slightly obscured view of the street.

My fellow Singaporeans are outraged.

The bus stop has thick pillars, which make it difficult to see approaching buses.

The bus stop is narrower than most, which makes it difficult to move around.

The bus stop has brought shame upon the country.

So I was packed off to Punggol to find as many angry passengers as possible.

The bus stop was certainly weird. It was built away from the nearby drains, which reduced the space, and the long line of pillars was big enough to prop up the Parthenon.

But if I stood up, I saw the buses just fine. Apparently, that was the problem. An auntie, sitting on a bench and leaning on her shopping trolley, laid out her daily drama for me.

'Cannot see the buses from here, right?' she said.

'No, but you can if you stand up.' I pointed at a bus heading towards us. 'I can see that one.'

She tutted at me. Clearly, I was a moron. She said, 'Yah *lah*, but if not my bus, then how?'

I said, 'You can sit down again?'

'Waste my time for what?'

Several bus stop regulars agreed. Standing up to check on a bus, when it was not their bus, was not a productive use of their time.

According to the NDP song, we're supposed to stand up for Singapore. We won't even stand up for a bus.

One commuter wondered if I had any idea how troublesome it was to constantly peer around a pillar to see if the right bus was coming.

I really didn't.

I asked if he had considered standing further away from the pillars, which would give him an unobstructed view of the road for at least a hundred metres or so. He shook his head in disbelief. I was asking him to consider standing in an area just outside of the sheltered walkway.

You'd think I'd asked him to stand in an area just outside of Chernobyl.

Back in the newsroom, I called all the relevant parties for their meaningless quotes about the troublesome bus stop.

A representative for the Member of Parliament promised to investigate the residents' 'feedbacks'.

A representative for the National Parks Board had no comment to make, as the bus stop did not fall within NParks' purview but sent me a glossy PDF of their plans to add greenery to bus stop rooftops, which had no relevance whatsoever. But the pictures looked nice.

A representative for the architecture firm behind the bus stop's design referred me to the Land Transport Authority.

A representative for the Land Transport Authority promised to consider 'architectural improvements to the existing infrastructure, whilst balancing the underlying limitations of the location and the adjacent utility operations.'

I had no idea what the quote meant. Nor did Peranakan Pervert. Nor did Uncle Groper.

Nevertheless, Mother Superior insisted that the quote be published as it was. She didn't know what the quote meant either.

Day 39

My bus stop story has so far generated two hundred and forty-eight comments on our Facebook page alone. The anti-government camp believed that the poorly designed bus stop was indicative of out-of-touch policy makers who never took public transport.

The pro-government camp believed that the story was the whiny, woke nit-picking of an air-conditioned nation.

And a couple of guys got into a lengthy debate about my

photo byline, agreeing that I was hotter than Lauren Lam but my '*neh neh* probably not so nice'. They were right about my *neh neh*. I was impressed by their intuition. You can't see my *neh neh* in my photo byline.

Day 40

A prominent politician shared my bus stop non-story on Facebook today. Captain Mayhem was delighted. He went to school with that prominent politician.

Day 41

My bus stop non-story was discussed in Parliament today. A young, idealistic MP highlighted the need to put the public's interest first in all public transport infrastructure.

He mentioned my name in Parliament.

My mother told her mahjong friends. My father sat me down and warned me of the dangers of getting involved with the Singapore Government.

His voice never rose above a whisper, just in case.

We were sitting in our own living room.

Day 42

In response to yesterday's enquiries from the young, idealistic MP, an older MP produced his preliminary findings about the problematic bus stop in Punggol. According to the report, a standing commuter had 12.7 seconds, on average, to see an approaching bus. But a sitting commuter had only 4.6 seconds, on average, to see an approaching bus between the pillars.

The young, idealistic MP wondered if the viewing times for sitting commuters might be improved with minor, cost-effective adjustments to the bus stop's design. The older MP assured the young, idealistic MP that he had commissioned a study on a bus stop redesign and welcomed public feedback.

This parliamentary debate led our TV news tonight. For a full three minutes. The second story came from Ukraine, where forensic experts had exhumed hundreds of bodies, including children, at a mass burial site.

Day 43

Slick Scholar sent out an email to all journalists today. We are expected to submit ideas for stories around an upcoming World News Day special.

I quietly asked Uncle Groper to tell me what World News Day meant.

He said, 'Slow news day.'

Day 44

After spending last night reading up on World News Day, I discovered the following:

World News Day is a global campaign to amplify the power of fact-based journalism.

World News Day celebrates the value of trustworthy journalism.

World News Day protects the rights of journalists to operate freely.

World News Day recognises the crucial role that journalists play in society.

I arrived at my cubicle feeling inspired, ready for my Jerry Maguire moment. I hammered out a couple of pages on the despicable treatment of migrant workers in our society, herding them like cattle on open trucks and locking them away in prison-like dormitories during the pandemic.

I was going to tick every one of World News Day's boxes.

Peranakan Pervert said no.

He read my ideas, sipped his coffee, and said, 'No need to talk about such sensitive issues.'

I said, 'Isn't that what World News Day is for?'

He almost spat out his coffee. He said, 'No *lah*, it's to win awards.'

Peranakan Pervert then complimented me on my new haircut, so the day wasn't a total loss.

Day 45

Peranakan Pervert must have felt bad this morning. He gave me a proper, fact-based piece to write on the eve of World News Day.

I compiled a top ten list of restaurants with the best views of the Singapore Grand Prix.

Day 46

Today is World News Day.

Slick Scholar wrote a lengthy editorial espousing the importance of investigative journalism in society, leaving no stone unturned in our quest for the truth. It was stirring stuff.

Then he was called to a meeting with government officials to go through the new media guidelines.

Day 47

Uncle Groper thanked me for my incisive reporting on the best vantage points to watch blurred vehicles in the Singapore Grand Prix.

He had dined at the No.1 restaurant on my list and informed the manager that he had sub-edited the piece. The manager had given him a free bottle of wine. Uncle Groper was still hung over.

He said, 'The *makan* there damn *shiok*, Millie.'

I said, 'I cannot afford to eat at these places. Don't earn as much money as you.'

He said, 'You don't know as much about editing as me.'

I agreed. We giggled. He belched. He gave me a whiff of last night's wine.

After the evening conference, Slick Scholar and Captain Mayhem came down to our newsroom. They were like debt collectors. If they turned up together, it had to be bad news.

Slick Scholar had tucked in his shirt. Captain Mayhem was wearing a tie. It was *very* serious.

Slick Scholar went first. He said, 'Sorry to interrupt, but we have an announcement to make. It's never easy to make these announcements.'

He appeared to sigh. His innate self-confidence, which only comes with the best education that a social network can buy, had deserted him. He even looked down at the carpet. Slick Scholar always gave intense eye contact. That was his thing. He never turned away. He never even blinked. Instead, he left you gazing at his perfectly parted hair and square jaw, almost daring you to look away. But he only had eyes for the office carpet now, leaving Captain Mayhem to take over.

'We're going through a period of transition,' the CEO said quickly. He was all business.

He stepped in front of Slick Scholar. 'And these decisions are never easy. But the media industry is facing unique challenges in a tough economic climate.' For the first time, I realised he was holding a white envelope. Where did it come from? Did Slick Scholar pass it to him? Was this a magic trick?

Captain Mayhem said, 'We have to make difficult changes, as we adjust to the rapidly evolving demands of digital media. But it's important to reward those who helped us along the way.'

I realised where they were standing now.

I knew what the envelope was for. I knew who it was for.

Captain Mayhem smiled and said, 'Uncle Groper ...'

Uncle Groper was already on his feet, loyal to the end. For a second, I thought he was going to salute the pair of them. Or punch them. It was always hard to tell with Uncle Groper.

Captain Mayhem held out a white envelope for the last check sub in the building. He said, 'You have been with us for almost thirty years, Uncle Groper.'

'Thirty-two years,' Uncle Groper muttered.

'That's right,' said the CEO. 'And I know the great work you've done in those thirty-two years.'

Captain Mayhem has been with our media company for five months.

'So do I,' added Slick Scholar.

Slick Scholar was a toddler 32 years ago.

Captain Mayhem held out the white envelope and said, 'It's only right and fair that your work is rewarded. Don't worry this is not an $8 *hong bao*.'

Half the room laughed loudly at the crass joke, the half that never wanted a white envelope.

The other half stood in silence, the half that knew that Uncle Groper never wanted a white envelope either.

He hesitated. His horrified face suggested the white envelope was covered in anthrax.

Captain Mayhem said, '*Aiyah*, don't be modest. You've given us thirty-two years. So, we've given you enough to enjoy the retirement you deserve with your grandkids.' Uncle Groper didn't have grandkids. He wasn't even married. He just had the job and lifelong self-denial. Now he only had self-denial.

Captain Mayhem pushed the white envelope into Uncle Groper's hand. Our CEO started applauding, loudly, before Uncle Groper had fully taken the white envelope. Slick Scholar followed his boss, slapping his hands together like a seal at feeding time.

Slick Scholar stretched out his arms and moved his clapping hands from left to right, encouraging others to join in.

Half the room applauded immediately and loudly. The other half applauded slowly and quietly, the half fearing a similarly fake ovation was coming for them. As an additional *reward* for his long and loyal service, Uncle Groper didn't have to finish the working day. He could leave whenever he wanted, presumably after he had said his goodbyes but before there was any chance of making a scene.

Naturally, Uncle Groper refused to leave until he had put the product to bed, one last time.

He edited my copy, wrote a few headlines, made some half-hearted sex puns with Peranakan Pervert and Hokkien Half-Ball, hugged his old colleagues and left. Once his desk was cleared, it was like he was never there.

Day 48

Captain Mayhem called a town hall meeting for all editorial stuff. Attendance was compulsory unless there was a compelling excuse.

Hokkien Half-Ball called me to say that he had a compelling excuse. I could hear his compelling excuse in the background, taking his money at her Singapore Pools counter.

Captain Mayhem was a short guy, making it hard for the journalists at the back of the newsroom to see him. Slick Scholar provided a stool for the CEO to stand on. He towered over us now, with a large head and a squat body. He looked like a Funko Pop doll.

He said, 'I know there's been a fair bit of discussion about the latest round of retrenchments. So I said to Slick Scholar, let's get everyone together, hear your concerns and address them. Full transparency. Any questions?'

Dozens of hands went up, which was unusual for a room filled with Singaporean journalists.

Lauren went first, asking if they'd be more retrenchments in the future.

'I cannot say,' said Captain Mayhem.

A guy from sales asked how the retrenched people were selected. He looked sweaty and jittery. The sales department were not hitting their targets.

'I cannot say,' said Captain Mayhem.

Peranakan Pervert tried his luck. He said, 'When will a decision be made about the next round of retrenchments?'

'I cannot say,' said Captain Mayhem.

Peranakan Pervert persisted. He said, 'But they said the previous round was going to be the last round of retrenchments and then people like Uncle Groper had to go.'

'It's always sad to see excellent writers like Uncle Groper leave the company,' said Captain Mayhem.

'He was a sub-editor,' said Peranakan Pervert.

'Exactly. And a very good one. Now, do you have any more questions?'

'You haven't answered any yet.'

That one was me. Stupidly.

I felt Lauren squeezing my elbow skin, which was weird. 'Don't,' she hissed.

Captain Mayhem was not amused. 'I've been as forthcoming as I can be, Millie.'

I said, 'Uncle Groper was asked to leave immediately, after working here for thirty-two years.'

Captain Mayhem nodded enthusiastically, to show everyone how much he agreed with me. He almost fell off his stool.

'And we tried to reward that loyalty with a fair pay out.'

'It doesn't seem fair,' I said. But it came out wrong. I sounded too pouty, too teenage angsty, like a spoiled brat not getting extra chicken wings for dinner.

'It isn't fair, Millie,' snapped Captain Mayhem. He was really wobbling on that stool. 'It isn't fair that the younger generation doesn't read local news anymore.'

Slick Scholar tried to intervene. He said, 'Well, we should probably go back and get our story ideas in for the evening conference now.'

'No, wait first,' Captain Mayhem interjected. 'This is

important. I'm not the bad guy here. Traditional media in every country has been disrupted forever. And your generation disrupted it. My generation, Uncle Groper's generation, we kept it going for decades. But now it's gone. Our old business model was not sustainable. Young people will pay six bucks for a frozen yoghurt but won't pay anything for journalism. That's the reality for all of us. I didn't smash local media. I'm trying to save it. And I understand your anger, Millie, I really do. All of you. You are young journalists at the beginning of your careers coming in at the end of something. And I'm here to help you. Your job is to produce quality journalism every day. I don't know how to do that. My job is to make sure our company stays solvent. I do know how to do that. I've been doing that for forty years. And I will do that. For all of you.'

The applause was spontaneous and genuine. Lauren and I glanced at each other and giggled, as if we couldn't quite believe we were clapping along. Without saying a word, Lauren and I shared a moment of clarity. We were going to do our best work for the man on the stool. We were going to win awards for the man on the stool. We were going to save Singapore media for the man on the stool.

'Because if I don't do my job,' Captain Mayhem continued. 'If I don't hit the right numbers, then there may be another retrenchment exercise at Christmas.'

We stopped clapping. We wanted to kick the man off the stool.

Luckily, Captain Mayhem's job didn't involve reading the room. He climbed down from his stool in silence.

Once our CEO had left, Slick Scholar reminded us that our

town hall meetings were confidential. We were instructed not to leak anything later.

We were professional journalists. We didn't need to be told.

Live updates from the town hall meeting had already been leaked on social media.

Day 49

After work, Hokkien Half-Ball took us to a rooftop bar overlooking the final preparations for the Singapore Grand Prix. Apparently, Hokkien Half-Ball did his National Service with the manager and we were very lucky to get in. The bar was hosting 'a premium F1 event'. Walk-ins were not allowed. It was a typical Marina Bay venue on the eve of the Singapore Grand Prix. We were the only Singaporean customers in the bar.

In our corner, Uncle Groper was holding court, telling the old stories. We heard the one about the wealthy businesswoman who had final approval for all her photographs, the one about the tough editor who burst into tears after a ministerial dressing down and the one about the editor who kept a Bat-phone that put him straight through to the Istana.

Who knew if these stories were true?

I was discovering that our instinctive self-censorship in the newsroom was built on an Orwellian myth. *They* were always watching. *They* had ISD spies on every floor. There was a Bat-phone, for god's sake. Who were these spies? Where were they watching us from? Where was this Bat-phone? It didn't matter.

The myths prevailed. The fear sustained itself.

On my way to the ladies, an American banker complimented me on my 'awesome hair' and offered to buy me a drink, at an event that came with a free flow of champagne. I considered his generous offer. He obviously used his gym membership. He had the high hair quiff and the shaved sides that every *ang moh* seemed to have these days. He kept jutting out his left arm, presumably to show me the expensive watch he was wearing.

He said something about being a corporate trainer, which sounded really well paid and really boring. He was good looking though, in a half-price Ryan Gosling kind of way.

'Yeah, OK,' I said. 'But I'll go to the toilet first?'

He found me hilarious. I wasn't. But he was drunk and my dress was tight. He kept laughing, until he threw up over my shoes.

I just stood there, speechless, as his warm vomit slipped between my toes.

'Hey, *ang moh*, fuck off, eh?'

Hokkien Half-Ball was suddenly standing beside me, pushing the corporate trainer aside and handing me some tissues.

Day 50

There was a sweaty lump in my bed this morning. He rolled towards me and said, 'We've got to stop doing this, eh?'

Hokkien Half-Ball laughed at his own joke. I watched him scratch the Liverpool tattoo on his upper arm. I didn't know what to say. I didn't really know where I was. Hokkien Half-Ball checked his watch and informed me that he still had time for a quick one before a morning meeting.

I politely declined. My hangover was kicking in. I felt nauseous and last night's vomit still lingered. I really had to dump those shoes later.

Hokkien Half-Ball kissed me on the cheek, reminded me to put my storylines into the schedule and insisted on paying for the Hotel 81 room.

Who says romance is dead?

At the office, Peranakan Pervert asked for a 'supervisory chat' in the meeting room. He looked even more anxious than usual. I wasn't particularly surprised. Captain Mayhem's retrenchment exercises were working their way through the old guard. Uncle Groper was in his sixties. Peranakan Pervert was in his late fifties. We could all do the maths.

In the meeting room, my supervisor told me to take a chair with a more abrupt tone than usual. The tips of his fringe were sweaty. He closed the door behind me and checked the newsroom. Our meeting room was essentially a goldfish bowl. Walls of glass from floor to ceiling supposedly gave the impression of full transparency. There were no secrets in our office. And no hidden corners to shag each other, like the good old days, when *ah pek* editors thought 'Me Too' meant that they could take turns to shag the interns.

No one was paying attention to our meeting. Why would they? Reporters debriefed news editors all the time. This was a completely normal meeting to have. Peranakan Pervert opened his laptop. He had two online tabs splitting the screen. My F1 lifestyle story was on the left. An F1 lifestyle story from a rival news agency was on the right.

He tapped my story and said, 'Millie, I asked you to get the most extravagant F1 package.'

I thought that I had.

'No, this guy did.' Peranakan Pervert tapped the other story. 'This package involves private jets, suites at Marina Bay Sands, nights at the Paddock Club. This one sounds really prestigious.'

I said they all sounded tacky.

'Exactly,' said Peranakan Pervert. 'It comes across in your writing. Your quirky tone works for the feature pieces, but you're sneering at your audience here. We have to get behind the grand prix.'

'Why?'

'Because it makes a lot of money.'

'For who?'

Peranakan Pervert closed his laptop and said, 'Am I being interviewed now?'

I apologised. I had woken up on the right side of the bed in the wrong hotel. My supervisor patted my hand and said, 'Millie, you're doing really well. You're probably one of the best probationary reporters we've had. You're smart. Intuitive. Hard-working.'

I expressed my gratitude.

He said, 'But this thing with Hokkien Half-Ball? Come on ah.'

Now I was sweating. But I wasn't sure why. Or I wasn't sure of my emotion at least. I was embarrassed, obviously. I was certainly self-conscious of my appearance. I knew I was blushing. But I think I was angry, too, which didn't help the hangover and my dodgy stomach.

I told Peranakan Pervert that I didn't understand.

He pointed towards the newsroom and said, 'Everyone knows Hokkien Half-Ball. He's a character *lah*. He's cheeky, funny. He's my good friend. But you are still on probation.'

Now I knew I was angry. Hokkien Half-Ball was clearly bragging about his sexual conquests like a bloody student. But more than that, we were consenting adults. So I pushed back.

'Sorry, why does my probation matter? Outside of work is my business, right?'

Peranakan Pervert pulled a face like he was constipated. 'Yes and no,' he said. 'The company is wary of these situations. Supervisors. Vulnerable reporters. Our track record has not been great with these tricky relationships.'

'It's not a relationship,' I insisted. 'It's just, well, it's nothing. It's between me and him.'

'Understood.'

Peranakan Pervert rolled his chair towards me. He stared into my bloodshot eyes and patted my hand a second time. He said, 'Hokkien Half-Ball has already given me his side of the story.'

Suddenly, I was grateful for the goldfish bowl. I was grateful for the prying eyes. I wanted every *kaypoh* face in Singapore peering into our meeting room. Peranakan Pervert's hand was still on top of mine. He said, 'It'll be fine.'

'What does that mean?'

'It means I'll settle it for you.'

I pulled my hand away. I tried to edge my seat away, too, but a roller hit another chair. I couldn't move. I was too close. I could smell the *bak chor mee* on his breath. I wanted to know what needed settling.

He said, 'I need to settle this with Slick Scholar. Look. Let's have a drink after work. I'll talk you through the process.'

'No need. Thanks.'

Peranakan Pervert reached for my hand again. He said, 'I'm just trying to help you and your career. We'll discuss it over drinks.'

'OK. Thanks.'

I left the room.

But I didn't meet Peranakan Pervert for drinks. I ignored him for the rest of the day. I just watched him later that evening, through the glass, eating with Hokkien Half-Ball at the same meeting table, as they scooped handfuls of *nasi padang* into their giggling mouths.

I didn't say anything to anyone, not even Lauren.

I didn't even comment when Peranakan Pervert sent my F1 lifestyle piece to Slick Scholar, comparing it unfavourably to a rival news agency.

I didn't say a word. How could I? I was still on probation.

Day 51

Lauren asked me to be her 'plus one' at a Family Fun Day. Our media organisation was a sponsor. And she'd been asked to file a fluff piece on the event. It was my day off, but my mother was playing mahjong with her friends, and I didn't fancy another interrogation about my sex life.

Lauren was also single. She didn't fancy random interrogations about her sex life at the Family Fun Day. The sponsors had very traditional views on love and marriage. They believed only in men and women. Lauren and I had considered wearing rainbow tops and holding hands, but our media organisation was a sponsor. This Family Fun Day was like *The Truman Show* with Singaporean actors. Smiling volunteers handed out balloons and popcorn to smiling, painted faces. There were Uncle Ringo's rides, cups of corn and cheese tofu. There was Captain Mayhem giving out free drinks.

Our bosses volunteered because our media organisation was a sponsor. One of our board members was giving a free talk on the importance of strengthening family bonds within the home. He'd recently found religion.

According to Lauren, he'd found religion at a very specific moment in his life, when his wife had found his mistress' earring in the family's Lexus.

The wife stood beside her husband at the stage, wearing a new Rolex. As we walked through the crowd, Lauren pointed out all the editors she suspected of cheating on their wives.

She figured the number was around twenty per cent, a definite decline since Harvey Weinstein had spoiled the market and blurred the lines for everyone. I liked Lauren. We were becoming a safe space for each other, a chance to gossip about dirty old men and blur reporters behaving like concubines. Naturally, I didn't mention Hokkien Half-Ball, in case Lauren got the wrong idea.

After too much cotton candy and chrysanthemum tea, she'd

scribbled down more than enough asinine quotes for her short piece, but we hung around for the event's pièce de resistance. Children had gathered with wet sponges to throw at victims in the dunking chair.

Captain Mayhem was sitting in the dunking chair because our media organisation was a sponsor.

The photo would almost certainly be included alongside Lauren's piece. We joined the cheering crowd of kids, and I soon felt a soggy object on my foot. A breathless boy ran towards me. 'I drop my sponge,' he said.

'It's all right,' I said, picking it up from my drenched toes.

What is it with strangers spilling stuff on my toes?

The boy's mortified mother had appeared. She was pushing a covered buggy. A baby girl snoozed inside. 'I'm so sorry,' she said.

'No problem,' I said, handing the sponge to her son, who disappeared into the crowd.

The mother snapped her head back and said, 'You were supposed to be watching him.'

'I was,' the father shouted through the crowd.

But he wasn't paying attention. He was typing on his phone, until he wasn't.

'Oh fuck,' said Hokkien Half-Ball.

He apologised for the language, blaming it on his son for soaking my feet. He introduced me to his wife. I shook her hand and smiled. I wished her family a fun day at the Family Fun Day. I had to. Our media organisation was a sponsor.

Day 52

I woke up to nine missed calls. Hokkien Half-Ball called again while I was eating porridge. I ignored him and went back to reading Lauren's story about the wholesome Family Fun Day.

On the MRT, I ignored the tenth and eleventh calls from Hokkien Half-Ball. I was about to get off the train when I realised that he hadn't left any voice messages or text messages. Initially, I appreciated his sensitivity. He wanted to speak to me directly.

Heading up the escalators, I was annoyed by my naivety.

Text and voice messages could be forwarded. They were evidence. In the office, I was convinced that every topic of conversation in every cubicle involved my name.

I was a cliché now. *The office slut.*

Lauren bought me a coffee and rambled on about the editing of her piece. Apparently, Captain Mayhem had rejected seven photos of himself sitting on the dunking stool, before settling on one that obscured his potbelly.

Her inane bitching helped though. She obviously didn't know about me and Hokkien Half-Ball.

In our desk meeting, Peranakan Pervert handed me a live grenade. He wanted a follow-up piece on gay activists challenging the legal definition of marriage in Singapore.

He told me to make some calls and bring my ideas to the evening conference. He didn't really make eye contact. He obviously did know about me and Hokkien Half-Ball and this was his childish revenge.

Any story on gay activism was a poisoned chalice. And Peranakan Pervert knew that.

At the evening conference, I felt surrounded. The foreign and finance desks where there, but I didn't care about them.

He was in the room.

Hokkien Half-Ball sat beside Peranakan Pervert, showing the latest betting odds on his phone. The pair chuckled like fucking schoolboys.

I was squeezed in next to Mother Superior. Her scribbling sounded like nails on a chalkboard. The grammar Nazi seemed more unhinged than usual. Her scrawl was more manic. Red ink covered her pages. Was she making a point to me? Did she know? My paranoia was off the charts.

Slick Scholar joined us last, taking his usual seat at the head of the mahogany table. He smiled at me first. He had to know surely.

'Ah, glad to see you here today, Millie,' he said.

I was in no doubt now. Slick Scholar definitely knew about me, Hokkien Half-Ball and the poor, oblivious wife. Slick Scholar was practically calling me a whore under his breath.

They all were. My withering brain couldn't handle the screaming voices. So I avoided eye contact. I kept my head down as the editors went through their major stories. Now the Formula One circus had moved on, Slick Scholar liked the idea of a reflective piece on the carbon footprint left behind.

Such a delicate issue could be discussed now. The F1 money had already been made.

In sport, they were going to lead with something to do with

English football, because local football was not popular.

In lifestyle, they had a feature on Taylor Swift's ticket prices, because local music was not popular.

And the Singapore desk was doing a piece on work visas because foreigners were not popular.

Once the day's stories were settled, the evening conference moved on to the weekend's long reads. These were our in-depth features about topical issues. They were less time sensitive and enjoyed a longer shelf life, which pleased potential advertisers.

We needed to please potential advertisers. The decision had been made to produce more provocative reads: smart, socially relevant and easy clickbait. I had been given marriage and gay activism in Singapore. I was screwed. Peranakan Pervert really hadn't forgiven me for rejecting his 'drinks' offer.

Slick Scholar seemed supportive though. He said, 'What have you got so far, Millie?'

I felt all their eyes now, except his. Hokkien Half-Ball scrolled through his phone.

I focused on my notepad and said, 'OK, I've spoken to a couple of Singaporeans who got married in San Francisco and want to renew their vows here.'

Mother Superior visibly shuddered. 'They are men?'

'Yes, a lawyer and a doctor,' I said. 'They want to ...'

'Cannot,' interrupted Mother Superior.

'Yeah, I know they cannot get married,' I continued. 'I'm just going to ...'

'No, you cannot,' she interrupted again.

I pictured stabbing her in the eye with her red pen. It didn't help.

I asked what it was that I couldn't do.

'You cannot interview gay men for this piece,' said Mother Superior, firmly.

I reminded her that the entire piece was supposed to be about gay men.

'Cannot,' she said. 'Juxtaposition.'

I looked to Slick Scholar for guidance. For anything. He nodded kindly and said, 'What Mother Superior means is, we cannot be seen to be advocating an alternative lifestyle. The media guidelines are clear on that.'

'Exactly,' said Mother Superior. 'You put two married gay men in this story. It looks like you are supporting gay marriage. Juxtaposition.'

She went back to tearing an intern's copy to pieces.

I was completely lost now. 'But the story is about two gay men, challenging a constitutional amendment that stops gay men from marrying and I can't talk to gay men? Who can I talk to?'

'Straight men,' said Slick Scholar.

'For a story about gay men?'

'And women. Talk to women, also,' said Slick Scholar. 'Let's get both sides.'

'Exactly,' agreed Mother Superior.

Slick Scholar said, 'We know how the gay community feels about this constitutional challenge. Let's get some alternative views from the straight community.'

'The straight community?' I asked.

'It'll give you the other side.'

'Can I speak to lesbians?'

I could see that I was testing Slick Scholar's patience. He said,

'No, Millie. Just a fair balance of views. This one we cannot fight.'

'No gay perspective at all?'

'Not until things settle,' said Slick Scholar.

'No juxtaposition,' said Mother Superior.

I said, 'OK, so no gay men in a story about gay men that only affects gay men?'

'Juxtaposition,' said the broken record.

Slick Scholar was eager to move on. He said, 'Look, it's tricky. But Peranakan Pervert put you forward for this one. So maybe take this offline with him?'

Peranakan Pervert grinned and said, 'Yeah. I'll take care of her.'

After the meeting, Peranakan Pervert sauntered over to my cubicle. He leaned over the partition. Most of us had partitions. We were like battery hens, laying one approved press release after another.

Peranakan Pervert tilted his head to one side, like a puppy. He was showing me how supportive he was, ready to listen. He was concerned about me. I had seemed a 'bit off' in the evening conference, apparently.

He wanted to reassure me that he was there for me. He reassured me by leaning over the partition, rubbing my back and peering down at my cleavage. I felt *so* reassured.

The funny thing about Peranakan Pervert was, he didn't even pretend. He was a committed bachelor. No wife. No hypocrisy. According to Lauren, he spent his days chasing young, gullible reporters and his nights at massage parlours.

He asked if I needed anything.

Yes. I needed him to stop rubbing my back.

He asked if he could help in any way.

Yes. He could remove his fingertips from my bra strap.

He asked if I wanted anything to be clarified.

Yes. The office guidelines on sexual harassment.

Naturally, I said nothing. I shook my head and played the diligent Asian on probation. 'Go and speak to Equality Matters,' he said.

His unexpected instruction caught me off guard.

'For the gay activism piece,' he added. 'Equality Matters will know what to say.' My supervisor finally pulled his hand away. Other reporters were wandering past my desk.

I said, 'Aren't Equality Matters considered activists, too?'

'*Yah lah*, the acceptable face of activism. They'll give a statement on marriage equality, but they won't be radical,' said Peranakan Pervert.

He turned his head and smiled at a passing intern. Her top was low. She was also a junior college student. Peranakan Pervert waited for her to leave the newsroom before returning to my breasts.

He said, 'Get some quotes from Equality Matters and then we'll have a drink after work to discuss the piece.'

His hand was back on my shoulder, rubbing its way towards my bra strap.

'I'm busy tonight,' I said.

'You really need to finish this feature, before your time on the news desk ends.' Peranakan Pervert showed me his cheap watch. 'Time is running out.'

'OK, I'll rush back to the office afterwards.'

'No need. I'll be in the coffee shop by then. Let's meet there?'

The tip of his middle finger burrowed its way beneath the bra stap, digging against my skin. I'd had enough. 'I don't wanna have a drink with you,' I snapped.

He leered back at me. 'And I don't wanna tell Hokkien Half-Ball's wife about you.'

Day 53

I was in no mood to visit the Equality Matters Centre. I felt like a total fraud. The centre investigated and defended women's rights. But I hadn't defended myself when my supervisor had assumed the right to investigate my bra strap. I met with the vice-president of the organisation, which only made me feel worse. She had devoted most of her adult life to causes around gender equality. What had I done? I had taken the Feminist Studies course at NTU and attended discussions on women's rights in Singapore when she was on the panels. I had even written an explainer in the *Nanyang Chronicle* about J.K. Rowling and the rise of trans exclusionary radical feminists, which wasn't easy. I had loved Harry Potter as a kid. And the Equality Matters Vice-President crushed me. Once I'd scribbled down her quotes on the definition of marriage in the Women's Charter (she wanted a more fluid definition) and the Constitution's intention to safeguard the traditional definition between a man and a woman (bad) and the constitutional challenges that will keep coming (good), she made me a cup of tea and did the worst thing imaginable.

She complimented me.

'I liked your article on that National Day dancer,' she said.

I seriously thought I might burst into tears. My self-esteem couldn't take compliments. I felt like a hypocrite.

The Equality Matters Vice-President helped low-income mothers, single parents and those trapped in violent and abusive relationships. I came from a traditional, but stable, Chinese family. I had earned a scholarship to one of the top media companies in Asia and was getting regular bylines. Why was I allowing my supervisor to touch me?

'Ah, thank you,' I croaked. My throat was on fire.

'Are you OK?'

Her concern made me feel worse. She was being sincere. She didn't want anything from me. She was offering kindness with no groping fingers attached. I suddenly couldn't remember the last time I'd heard a question that wasn't loaded. The questioner usually wanted to sleep with me, date me, criticise me or tear my work to shreds.

The Equality Matters Vice-President had probably met hundreds like me over the years: young, gifted and submissive. I was an Asian cliché. Madame Butterfly. Geisha girl. Probationary reporter. The names had changed, but not much else. They were still taking from us, like they were doing us a huge favour. And what was I doing about it? What could I do about it? The answer was the same either way.

I assured her that I was super busy at the office.

The Equality Matters Vice-President pretended that she believed me. She said, 'I used to have friends in the media. Tough to be a female journalist in Singapore. It was even worse last time.'

'The sexism?' I asked.

She laughed and said, 'No, the shagging.'

I wondered what she'd heard.

She said, 'I've had so many of them come to me, in private. The wives. The mistresses. The girlfriends. So many over the years. They all had a different story, of course, depending on their status. But it must be better now, right?'

She was probing me. I could see that, just as she could see the curse of my father's DNA. He couldn't hide his drinking from my mother. And I couldn't hide my embarrassment from strangers. Our red cheeks gave us away.

'I've heard the rumours that it still goes on,' I muttered.

I was being the good Asian girl again, loyal to my rice bowl.

The Equality Matters Vice-President said, 'It's a company perk in Asia. A boss. A mistress. We are what we are.'

I said, 'Why ah?'

'Why what? What are you asking me? Why are we still accepting this?' The Equality Matters Vice-President found her own questions amusing. 'I'd ask, "how the hell did we get this far"? It's ingrained in our culture. Confucius told wives to obey their husbands, no matter what. Chinese history tells us about nasty, greedy mistresses making life miserable for their emperors. Even the British allowed the Chinese to stock up on wives and concubines. Has the mistress culture ever really gone away?'

'Not unless my Dad really does think the seafood is better in Batam,' I mumbled.

The Equality Matters Vice-President clapped her hands together, warming to her theme. 'The mistress in Batam, the office intern, it's still men benefiting from a patriarchal society,' she said. 'It's still this idea of an extra woman being an extra bonus for male achievement, eh?'

I knew I was blushing again. I didn't need to say anything.

The Equality Matters Vice-President had seen dozens like me before. That was the annoying part. She knew exactly what I was, or what I was allowing myself to become. She could see it in my face.

When the interview finished, she offered to walk me to the lift.

'Have you read some of the stuff online?' She asked, as she pushed the lift button. 'There are young Singaporean writers like you doing some really strong pieces on women's issues.'

'Yeah,' I said.

'Anyway, good luck with your piece. And remember ...'

She held the lift door open for me. 'We're not an extra bonus for them.'

Day 54

Mother Superior made me revise my copy seventeen times. Every mention of 'gay', 'sex' and 'homosexuality' made her visibly wince. The single reference to 'gay couple' almost caused a convulsion. That adjectival description was included in a paragraph that mentioned a politician.

'Cannot,' she muttered. 'Juxtaposition.'

Eventually, she removed five 'homosexuals' and three 'gays' from the piece. 'Enough already,' she said.

Peranakan Pervert removed the Equality Matters Vice-

President's suggestion that the constitutional definition of marriage needed to be more fluid.

He also excised her quote that a more balanced analysis should involve all parties. 'That one cannot,' he said. 'Must keep it balanced.'

Continuing with the theme of balance, Slick Scholar asked me to find another vox pop, preferably from a younger person, someone who supported the existing legal definition of marriage. To save time, I called the son of an auntie in marketing who had Bible extracts taped to her desk.

Captain Mayhem approved the piece, only after he'd made several phone calls and then asked for the headline to be watered down. Twice.

Hokkien Half-Ball came over to congratulate me on the feature's 'sensitivity', whatever that meant, and promised to run a blurb for the story on the homepage. I told him to fuck off to his wife.

Peranakan Pervert reminded me that I still owed him a drink to discuss recent 'sensitive' incidents. I was blessed to be among such selfless, empathetic men.

I told him to fuck off to Hokkien Half-Ball's wife. I told him to tell her everything about me and Hokkien Half-Ball. I told him that I had absolutely nothing to hide. After my piece went online, Captain Mayhem called and asked if I'd like to join him upstairs for a celebratory drink.

I put the phone down.

Day 55

Slick Scholar sent me a gushing email today. He praised the objectivity of a feature about gay couples that included no gay couples.

After work, I called the Equality Matters Vice-President and told her everything. I could not stop talking. I could not stop crying.

I asked for advice.

She said, 'No need. You know what to do already.'

Then she added, 'Great piece on gay marriage, by the way. It was so *balanced*.'

After that, neither of us could stop laughing.

Day 56

In the morning, Captain Mayhem participated in a public panel discussion on the future of Singapore media. He was effusive in his praise for young journalists, insisting that they were well equipped to successfully navigate the transition from old to new media.

In the evening, five junior reporters handed in their resignations, citing a lack of positive guidance and career support. Only one of them had left for a better-paid job. He was going to work in his father's chicken rice stall.

Day 57

Lauren found me crying in the women's toilets. She didn't pry. She simply said, 'Whatever it is, we've all been there. You'll deal with it.'

I spent the afternoon focusing on my work, interviewing twelve-year-old students from my alma mater about dealing with the pressure of PSLE exams. Two of them burst into tears.

In the evening, I sent an email to both Peranakan Pervert and Slick Scholar, asking to bring my first probation assessment review forward by a couple of days. An upbeat Slick Scholar sent a quick reply, booking the meeting room for tomorrow.

Peranakan Pervert did not reply.

Day 58

Probation Assessment Review – News Media

Slick Scholar had gone with his signature GQ look. His hair was as polished as his black shoes. The tight, open-neck white shirt showed off his hours in the gym. The pressed trousers showed off his helper's hours in front of an ironing board. He offered me a warm smile as I took my seat. His teeth really were perfect. He maintained eye contact the whole time, which was a pleasant change. Peranakan Pervert usually chatted to my chest.

But not today.

He was pretending to read the notes on his laptop. He had to impress the much younger man sitting beside him at the long mahogany table. There were rumours of another retrenchment exercise before Christmas.

Peranakan Pervert had gone with his seedy boss look. The faded polo shirt came with a curry stain. His nicotine habit came with yellow fingers.

He said, 'OK, then, obviously, you've been busy in your first two months.'

'Very,' agreed Slick Scholar. 'You hit the ground running with your National Day scoop and haven't stopped since. Just maintain that momentum on the radio side and you'll be fine.'

Peranakan Pervert finally decided to look up at me. He frowned. I was wearing a buttoned-up blouse. He turned his nose up at me. He needed to trim those nasal hairs.

He said, 'Yes, there were some good stories. Let's look at the numbers.' He turned his laptop towards me and pointed towards a bar graph. 'Those three stories had decent page views.'

Those stories of mine had covered the best F1 restaurants, the bus stop with the restricted view and a very short piece about a man holding up a placard that read 'Free meals for the poor'.

The placard holder was investigated for the possible offence of public assembly without a permit.

The placard holder was suspected of being an anti-government socialist, calling for more left-wing, welfarist polices.

The placard holder was a chef. He was literally offering free meals for the poor. He may now be nominated for a National Day Award for his act of kindness.

Peranakan Pervert then showed us another graph. He said, 'In terms of page views, this was by far your best story.'

It wasn't. It was the story about the sunbathing woman.

But key words like 'sunbathing' and 'bikini' had ended up in some porn algorithm. Peranakan Pervert suggested that I needed to write more stories like that.

I said, 'Stories for dirty old men?'

Slick Scholar cut in quickly. He said, 'He just means stories that resonate. These ones will always cut through with the heartlanders. But she's done well *lah*, overall, right?'

He got a begrudging, half-nod from Peranakan Pervert.

'OK, then, keep it up in radio, Millie,' said Slick Scholar, pressing his palms against the polished surface. He was ready to leave. 'Is there anything you'd like to say?'

I thought about the question.

I thought about my rice bowl.

I thought about my mother thinking about my rice bowl.

I thought about my father thinking about his Batam trips.

I thought about Hokkien Half-Ball's sweet kid and oblivious wife.

I thought about Peranakan Pervert's clammy hand on my back and his 'drinks' threat.

I thought about Uncle Groper's empty office cubicle.

I thought about my empty office cubicle, if I made the wrong choice.

And I thought about my late-night writing at NTU, filing copy for the *Nanyang Chronicle*.

It's all I ever wanted to do. It's all I've ever wanted to be.

I said, 'Yeah, I slept with Hokkien Half-Ball.'

Now I had the unbroken eye contact of two men: one surprised, the other horrified.

'What?' Slick Scholar was spluttering.

'That's your business,' said Peranakan Pervert. 'No need to discuss private lives here.'

'Then why did you discuss it out there?' I pointed to the newsroom. 'Why did you threaten to tell Hokkien Half-Ball's wife if I didn't go out with you?'

For the first time, I saw Slick Scholar drop the *GQ* act. The practised smile was put away. An instinctive snarl emerged in its place. He said, 'What's going on?'

'We can talk about this after, Millie,' said Peranakan Pervert.

Now he felt panicked. He felt threatened. He felt powerless.

Welcome to my world, asshole.

'No, I'd prefer to talk about it now, with the editor,' I said, turning my attention to Slick Scholar. 'Yes, I slept with Hokkien Half-Ball. Outside. Two adults. That's it. I didn't know he was married. He never told me. I found out by accident. That was it, until Peranakan Pervert threatened me. He told me to go out with him or he'd tell Hokkien Half-Ball's wife and humiliate me. He blackmailed me. I turned him down. That's why he's giving me shit now.'

'Come on ah,' said Peranakan Pervert.

'Just stop,' interrupted Slick Scholar. His elbows were on the table. His hands were clasped. He bowed his head, as if preparing to pray. He was certainly muttering to himself.

'I don't believe this,' he said, before looking up at me. 'OK, Millie, could you give us five minutes please. I'll speak to you later.'

Slick Scholar did speak to me later, to inform me that Peranakan Pervert had been given a generous redundancy package.

He had already left the building. There were no speeches.

There wasn't even time for that drink.

Day 59

Hokkien Half-Ball took a day's no-paid leave. Apparently, there was a family emergency.

Day 60

I was packing up my desk today when Hokkien Half-Ball casually wandered over. He made sure no one else was within earshot. Just in case I made a scene. He wished me well in my next posting with our flagship English radio station. He offered me a hand. I shook it.

I was still on probation.

THE PROBATION

Part II: Radio Media

October – November

Day 62

At 5.30am, I staggered towards the cramped, musty radio studio of The Rojak Breakfast Show. The show went out every weekday morning from 6am to 9am. Most of the radio ads were spent here because listeners were tuning in from cars worth more than my parents' life savings.

The Rojak Breakfast Show was the jewel in our company's crown, our most prestigious media platform.

It was presented by Loud and Louder, two funky, fast-talking DJs with dyed streaky hair and tattooed arms.

They were both older than my dad.

In person, they looked like hip-hop artists from the nineties MTV channel. They were wearing more makeup than me – to host a radio show.

I stood sheepishly in the open door as the red light flashed above my head. The pair were standing on the other side of the studio desk, finishing off their pre-recorded segments.

Mr Loud hit some buttons on the console and, in a soft, buttery voice, said: 'Can't sleep at night? Then call the Pillow Palace. And enjoy a royal sleep. Every night.' His delivery was that usual mix of husky Singaporean and energetic American that's heard everywhere on local radio and nowhere else.

The red button went off and Mr Loud waved me into the studio. He said, 'Eh, Millie, right? Come in *lah*. Don't be shy.'

He sounded Singaporean now.

Mr Louder looked me up and down. 'We heard a lot about you,' he said.

'I hope it was positive,' I croaked. My voice was still in bed.

'No *lah*, cannot say.'

Mr Louder ushered me to a seat across from them. He was brasher and rougher than his colleague. His Singlish was more natural, too. 'OK, mus' finish this one first,' he said, pulling a mic towards him.

The red light came on. Mr Louder cleared his throat. 'Expect lengthy traffic delays at the Woodlands checkpoints this morning. Allow more time for your journey. This message was brought to you by the Land Transport Authority.'

His polished delivery was flawless. It was like listening to the voice of God.

The red light went off.

'Fuck *lah*. Same shit every day,' said Mr Louder.

He no longer sounded like the voice of God.

At 5.55am, Loud and Louder laid out my initial duties. I had to monitor the social media comments and highlight any posts worth mentioning on the show. I had to collect guests, if we had any, and make them feel comfortable. Eventually, I would produce elements of the show, provide research for the DJs and prepare questions for the guests.

'Don't worry, we'll look after you,' said Mr Loud.

'Yeah, we've been doing this for twenty years. We're almost professional,' added Mr Louder.

At 6.10am, Mr Loud mentioned an online story about a smelly Singapore Airlines passenger on a recent flight from Sydney.

Reading from the news article, Mr Loud said, 'Other passengers complained that the man was emitting too much gas in a confined space.'

Mr Louder started laughing.

At 6.11am, Mr Louder was still laughing.

At 6.12am, Mr Loud highlighted the global energy crisis and our rising fuel bills and wondered if the passenger's gas could be monetised.

Mr Louder started laughing again.

At 6.15am, Mr Loud invited listeners to send in their worst examples of foul odours in public places. As the DJs headed into a musical break, Mr Louder dedicated *Uptown Funk* to 'Farty Man and his Funky Smell' on the SIA flight.

Mr Loud threw his head back and roared with laughter.

At 6.16am, *Uptown Funk* began to play. The DJs killed their mics and instantly stopped laughing. Mr Loud sent his wife a text message, reminding her that their eldest kid had PSLE tuition after school. Mr Louder asked me to monitor our social media feeds for the 'best bad smell stories', reminding me only to pick the 'clean' best bad smell stories.

At 6.18am, I cut and pasted the following listeners' comments into a shared document for the DJs. They read as follows:

'Smelly fart in a lift is the worst.'

'Cannot *tahan* durian on MRT. So selfish.'

'One time, my fren' drop stink bomb in class.'

'Fish head in the rubbish chute.'

'Nothing smell as bad as the PAP.'

At 6.19am, the DJs decided not to use the listeners' comments and opted to riff on 'Farty Man and His Funky Smell' instead.

At 6.30am, Loud and Louder had agreed that Farty Man and His Funky Smell could be a Marvel series on Disney Plus or a rapper from the 1990s or the durian seller at Mr Louder's local wet market.

At 6.40am, The Rojak Breakfast Show audience was invited to send in lists of the worst smells in Singapore, informing half a million listeners that 'our new girl, Millie, will select your worst smells in Singapore'.

At 6.45am, I was instructed to delete a comment that simply said, 'Foreigners'.

At 6.46am, Loud and Louder abandoned the idea of listing the worst smells in Singapore and thought an improvised rap might be more appropriate for their audience instead.

At 7.05am, the news wrap included cruise missile strikes on Ukrainian cities, a new wave in Covid-19 cases and soaring inflation.

At 7.10am, Loud and Louder performed the following rap on the primetime Rojak Breakfast Show:

'Farty Man and His Funky Smell
Ended up on a plane from hell
He filled the cabin with a ball of gas
And left himself with a big, red rash
Passengers were sore after such a grind
But not as sore as his loud behind
So SIA withdrew his air miles
For farting across all their aisles.'

They were crying with laugher by the time they were done.

Crying.

But I was no less complicit.

I provided fart noises as percussion.

At 8am, I thought about my university thesis on the transformation of digital media as I typed out an online audience request to submit the next verses of Farty Man and His Funky Smell.

At 8.15am, the DJs reminded listeners why The Rojak Breakfast Show was the most popular radio show in Singapore.

'Anything can go in,' said Mr Loud.

'And anything can go out,' said Mr Louder.

'A bit like Farty Man and His Funky Smell,' shouted Mr Loud.

At 8.16am, the pair were still giggling as they played Phil Collins'

'In the Air Tonight'.

'Do you get it? Mr Loud wondered.

'It's in the air all right,' added Mr Louder, just in case there was anyone who really, really didn't get it.

But Mr Loud blew a raspberry over Phil Collins' opening lyrics anyway, just in case.

At 8.35am, the DJs generously allowed me to utter my first words on a national radio station. I was going to announce the winner of the silliest lyrics contest. I didn't want to. In fact, I had asked them not to, during the song break.

But they had insisted, as a reward for my fine work, cutting and pasting listeners' comments into their Google document.

So I waited for the Bon Jovi track to finish. I licked my lips and dragged a mic towards me. Mr Loud pointed at me.

The red light came on.

I took a deep breath and said, 'James Lim wins the Farty Man and the Funky Smell silly lyrics contest.'

In terms of historic public speeches, Neil Armstrong had his one small step. Martin Luther King had his dream. I had Farty Man and the Funky Smell silly lyrics. The DJs were already giggling as they cued the applause clip on the console. They stood up and bowed at me, repeatedly.

'We're not worthy, we're not worthy,' they said in unison.

I felt ridiculously silly.

It was the most fun I'd had in two months.

Day 63

After today's show, Loud and Louder and I were asked to see Smooth Voice in his office.

Smooth Voice was the station's director. He had one of the huskiest, most seductive voices I'd ever heard. He used to present Late-Night Love Songs and I remember my mother going a bit giggly in the kitchen whenever he introduced the next Whitney Houston ballad.

She preferred the Chinese stations, but she never missed Smooth Voice's Late-Night Love Songs. Whenever he spoke, she'd chop the cabbage really fast. Then my father would wander into the kitchen in his sweaty singlet. My mother would stop chopping the cabbage.

But I could see where my mother was coming from. Sitting across from Smooth Voice in his office, I was hearing those dulcet tones live for the first time and my belly went all warm and tingly.

Then he coughed, repeatedly, filling the air with stale nicotine.

Some voices are born. Smooth Voice's was made with two packets of Marlboro a day.

He was probably in his mid-fifties and didn't look a day older than sixty. He held up a piece of paper and said: 'You probably know why you're here.'

Mr Loud went first. 'Farts?'

'Of course *lah*, farts, what else,' said Smooth Voice. He was irritated. Smooth Voice was the station director. The Rojak Breakfast Show was his flagship production, the one that brought in the most revenue.

Loud and Louder had been on the air since I was in secondary school. And their act hadn't really changed since I was in secondary school. But they were unbelievably popular, in the way that movies about girls doing National Service were unbelievably popular.

I suspect they were popular with older men like my father. He found those National Service movies hilarious. Every Chinese New Year, he insisted on our extended family going to Golden Village to watch the latest 'comedy'. Every Chinese New Year, he was the only one in our extended family who laughed out loud. But my dad liked the Rojak Breakfast Show. So did Captain Mayhem. They were around the same age, the same age of most men in power in Singapore. I suppose the show's popularity was obvious really.

But our ageing population was a problem. The Rojak Breakfast Show was keeping listeners, but not advertisers. My father's generation was not overly interested in the latest iPhone.

So Smooth Voice had been hired to reduce the age of the average listener. He was a self-proclaimed pop culture geek and a music aficionado.

But he hadn't appeared regularly in front of a microphone since the Backstreet Boys were on the radio every day. Luckily for him, the Backstreet Boys were still on the radio every day.

Smooth Voice's job was to change that.

When he was rehired, he did one of those 'likes and dislikes' interviews with a digital lifestyle platform, which our company also happened to own, to hail his return to radio.

Smooth Voice's favourite band was Depeche Mode.

Smooth Voice's favourite song was 'Brother Louie' by Modern

Talking.

Smooth Voice's favourite gig was Richard Marx at the Star Theatre.

Smooth Voice was hired to make local radio appealing to Generation Z.

But his voice did make my mother go funny when she chopped her cabbage.

So, there was *that*.

Smooth Voice held up another piece of paper and said, 'There were thirty-eight farts and seventeen fartys on your show yesterday. They're all listed here.'

I pictured an intern listening back to our show and scribbling down all the derivatives of 'fart'.

Mr Loud shrugged and said, 'I thought it was funny.'

'Yeah, we had a great reaction on social media,' agreed Mr Louder.

I got the impression that this wasn't their first dressing down. They barely cared. Even Smooth Voice appeared to be going through the motions. He turned to me and said, 'What do you think?'

The eyes of three middle-aged men were upon me. I could see what Smooth Voice was doing. I was the targeted demographic. I had the latest iPhone. I bought cheap clothes on Shein and tried not to think about the company's labour and IP exploitations. I was the one expected to buy into the Farty Man and the Funky Smell vibe.

I was also on probation, working for two of the biggest names in the media business.

'I thought it was funny,' I said.

'Ah you see,' said Mr Loud, getting restless in his chair.

'At first,' I added.

'*Wah*, she *sabo* me on her first day,' said Mr Loud.

But he didn't appear angry.

'Let her speak *lah*,' said Mr Louder, tapping Mr Loud's hand.

Smooth Voice seemed intrigued. He said, 'Go on. It's Millie, right?'

I said, 'Yeah. I thought it was funny at first. The stuff about travelling on the plane, bad passengers. That was all relatable. But I thought the rap was a bit ...' I was looking over at Smooth Voice, but I could feel the DJs glaring at me.

'A bit what?' Smooth Voice demanded an answer.

'I'm probably the wrong audience,' I blabbered. 'My parents love the show.'

Mr Loud visibly grimaced at the mention of my parents. Mr Louder looked like he'd been shot in the gut.

'Never mind your parents,' said Smooth Voice. 'What do you think?'

'I thought it was a bit ... *childish*.'

I should have just bitten my tongue. I felt the air being sucked from Smooth Voice's office.

He stared at Loud and Louder. Loud and Louder stared at me. Then Loud and Louder stared at Smooth Voice. And then the three men roared with laughter. My cheeks were already reddening. I thought they were laughing at me.

'Of course it's childish,' said Mr Loud. 'We wrote a rap about a man farting on a plane. It was shit.'

Mr Louder leaned across and patted my shoulder, which I did not appreciate. He said, 'Millie, I have a law degree. But I have a good voice and a funny face so I make fart jokes and make more money than a lawyer. *Relak lah.*'

Smooth Voice settled the room. He said, 'Just be mindful. Not too many farts first thing in the morning, OK?'

Mr Loud was intrigued. He said, 'What's the appropriate number?'

I sat back as I watched two Singaporean celebrities, one of whom had a law degree, and a radio icon, who made my mother go giggly over her cabbage, discuss how many times the word *fart* could be discussed on a primetime family breakfast show. They settled on eight. Eight farts per episode. It felt like a lucky number. Not for me though. My duties now included keeping count of the number of farts per episode.

The DJs then left the meeting. They needed to prepare. The men behind the Farty Man and the Funky Smell were emceeing a symposium for an international bank in the evening.

Smooth Voice asked me to stay back for a moment.

Once we were alone, he reiterated my importance to the radio studio. Even though my initial tasks were mostly administrative, I needed to understand my value. I was a gatekeeper. I had to moderate the comments carefully and quickly. 'Yeah, I'll delete the fart posts,' I said, grinning.

'No, it was this one.' Smooth Voice found a piece of paper on his desk and read out the Facebook comment. '*Nothing smell as bad as the PAP.*'

Apparently, someone had seen the simile on Facebook.

Apparently, someone had contacted Smooth Voice.

Apparently, someone in the office had checked how long the comment had stayed online.

Apparently, I had taken one minute and twenty-seven seconds to delete the comment.

Apparently, one minute and twenty-seven seconds was considered too long for a comment comparing the party of government to a bad smell.

'How long do I have then?' I wondered.

'You just wanna remove these things before they explode,' said Smooth Voice. He made it sound like I worked in the bomb squad.

Smooth Voice told me not to overly stress over the issue. He said, 'If you see anything potentially problematic, just delete it. Better to be safe than sorry, right?'

Thankfully, we are still allowed eight farts per show.

Day 65

Captain Mayhem organised a working lunch today at a fancy restaurant, a sharing session with the Rojak Breakfast Show crew. He wanted a chance to get to know every member of the production, from the guy who wrote the news to the guy who gave the best career advice and the funny one who picked out the best local dishes.

Captain Mayhem wanted to wait until everyone had arrived before starting. Smooth Voice cleared a mouthful of nicotine-coated phlegm and quietly pointed out that everyone had already arrived.

The news writer was outsourced.

The career guy was outsourced (and paid in *exposure*).

And the cooking guy was also outsourced (and also paid in *exposure*). But Loud and Louder did do their own weather reports, which I wrote for them.

'Wah, you guys really are *rojak*,' said Captain Mayhem, clearly enjoying the company.

While we waited for our lunches to arrive, he decided to play an ice-breaker game. I thought I was back in primary school.

The CEO of our media organisation wanted to go around the room, inviting each person to say their name, their job title and their favourite song because 'we are in the music business after all, ha ha'.

Naturally, he went first.

'Hello, I'm Captain Mayhem, the CEO, and my favourite song is The Eagles' "Hotel California".'

'Hello, I'm Mr Loud, the co-host of the Rojak Breakfast Show, and my favourite song is Guns N Roses' "Sweet Child O' Mine".'

'Hello, I'm Mr Louder, the better-looking co-host of the Rojak Breakfast Show, and my favourite song is "Dancing Queen" by Abba.'

'Hello, I'm Smooth Voice, the station director and the best song from the best decade is "Brother Louie" by Smooth Talking. The original version, not the cheesy remix.'

'Yeah, 'cos the original is so cool,' said Mr Louder.

'Balls to you,' said Smooth Voice.

'Tell us your favourite, Millie,' said Captain Mayhem, far too eagerly.

'Er, yes, my name is Millie Lee and I'm, like, a trainee producer for the Rojak Breakfast Show and I quite like Harry Styles' "As It Was".'

There were lots of nods of approval around the room. Captain Mayhem seemed confused. He said, 'What's that one ah?'

'Big hit,' said Mr Loud. 'He was in a boyband last time.'

'Ah Westlife?'

There were lots of nods of approval around the room. Captain Mayhem was our CEO.

The handsome, suited man beside the CEO said, 'Right, OK, my turn. My name is Slick Scholar and I'm the national editor for online news, TV and radio. And my favourite song is "Yellow" by Coldplay.'

At the end of the table, a forty-something woman peered into her phone, not realising we were waiting with bated breath. Smooth Voice cleared his throat to get her attention. The woman looked up.

She said, 'Eh? My turn ah? OK, my name is Sales Guru, I work in the marketing department. I sell the ads on all our radio stations and music programmes. I don't really like pop music.'

But she did have a grade eight certificate for playing the piano.

After much persuasion, she decided that her favourite songs were the *Nocturnes* by Chopin.

Captain Mayhem said he was disappointed that the restaurant didn't have a piano. No one else was.

After the excruciating small talk between mouthfuls, Captain Mayhem laid out his grand plan for the future of radio. According to the most recent Nielsen Radio Survey, our numbers were down, across all English radio stations. Our Chinese stations were holding steady, presumably because my mother still needs

Mandopop to cut cabbage. But the English stations were losing a grip on their audiences.

Advertisers were more likely to spend on targeted advertising campaigns on social media, where they could zero in on a specific demographic.

Captain Mayhem looked around the lunch table for suggestions. Slick Scholar wondered if the music selections could be skewed to a younger crowd. Smooth Voice pointed out that their music libraries had been extensively road-tested. Whenever newer songs, groups or genres were trialled, the audience rejected them. Apparently, the Rojak Breakfast Song played a couple of EDM tracks recently and listeners went ape shit.

Captain Mayhem leaned over to Smooth Voice and discreetly enquired if these EDM tracks had anything to do with the Economic Development Board.

Smooth Voice said, 'Not unless they've started adding drumbeats to board meetings.'

Loud and Louder defended their territory, pointing out that their audience share had declined the least. They knew their listeners and what they wanted. 'It's not my fault that they still wanna listen to Guns N' Roses,' said Mr Loud. 'But if we keep playing it, and make a few silly jokes either side, they're happy.'

Slick Scholar believed that young people wanted more challenging content.

Smooth Voice believed that young people had no interest in radio content, full stop.

Sales Guru believed that young people were irrelevant because they lacked purchasing power.

Mr Loud believed that young people loved fart jokes.

Mr Louder believed that young people loved his raps. He was a big hit with the National Service crowd.

And Captain Mayhem still wanted to know what an EDM track was.

They ignored me, the only young person in the room, as they decided amongst themselves what young people wanted to hear on the radio.

Not that I had any clue.

The last time I touched a physical radio was when I visited the National Museum.

On the way out of the restaurant, Captain Mayhem grabbed me by the arm and told me I could pitch him ideas for the Rojak Breakfast Show any time. He was determined to make radio relevant for my generation.

He also asked me to make a list of Harry Styles' songs, including his early stuff with Westlife.

Day 66

Captain Mayhem thanked me for the comprehensive Harry Styles playlist on Spotify. He felt it was important to connect with younger Singaporeans.

On every car trip, his personal driver was going to play my selections.

Day 67

I had a dream last night that Harry Styles had reunited with One Direction, but the original members of the band had been replaced with Captain Mayhem, Smooth Voice and Loud and Louder.

They were all wearing drivers' uniforms and singing *As It Was* to an audience of one. Me.

Slick Scholar was a background dancer, just slightly out of step with the beat.

Sales Guru was sitting just behind them, playing a piano.

They kept asking me to join them, but I didn't know the words. They had changed the lyrics.

It was like a bad lip-sync battle. Nothing seemed to match.

A loud, rhythmic banging kept interrupting the performance.

It was my mother. She was standing just off-stage, chopping up a cabbage.

Day 69

I made my official on-air debut today. Loud and Louder allowed me to write and record the weather. My first announcement on the Rojak Breakfast Show went as follows:

> 'And today's weather will be mostly cloudy, with a top temperature of thirty-two degrees, with showers in the late afternoon.'

After the show, Loud and Louder presented me with a Rojak Breakfast Show umbrella for 'breaking my cherry' on air. I had to pose with the umbrella beside our station logo. The photo was shared on all our social media platforms.

A listener posted that I had a 'sexy voice' and suggested that the in-studio camera was lowered during the weather reports to show my 'full body'.

He was blocked for his suggestion. He was a pervert.

Captain Mayhem sent me an email, praising me for my 'seductive voice' and suggested that the in-studio camera was adjusted during the weather reports to capture my 'full frame'.

He was thanked for his suggestion. He is our CEO.

Day 70

Following my successful baptism of fire yesterday, I am now the designated weather reader. I wrote and presented the following report:

> 'And today's weather will be mostly cloudy, with a top temperature of thirty-one degrees, with showers in the evening.'

I love the variety of my work.

Day 71

We had thunderstorms all morning. I did a rain dance around the studio.

I didn't realise that Mr Louder was filming my spontaneous rain dance. I didn't know that Mr Loud had uploaded the clip onto the Rojak Breakfast Show's social media platforms until the comments started to come in.

Some thought I looked cute. One asked for my phone number. My mother sent me a WhatsApp, pointing out that I looked a bit fat.

During the show, Smooth Voice sent us a note. He loved my silly dancing segment – it wasn't meant to be a segment, but it was performing well on TikTok – and asked me to consider more interpretative dances for different weather patterns in the future. Loud and Louder were still laughing when they dedicated 'Purple Rain' to me.

Day 74

We got in serious political trouble today. The British Prime Minister was compared to a lettuce in a UK tabloid newspaper. Mr Loud shared the story on air and noticed that it was getting plenty of traction on social media. So Mr Louder improvised a whole thing about comparing world leaders with different foods and invited listeners to join in.

I compiled a list of the best suggestions after my 8am weather report (hot, cloudy, top temperature of 31 degrees, showers in the late afternoon) and Mr Loud read it on air.

The former American President was an orange, obviously.

The Russian leader was a durian because he was prickly and you wouldn't want to be trapped in a room with him.

The Australian Prime Minister was a banana because it was shaped like a boomerang.

Our listeners are not comedy writers.

And Singapore's Prime Minister was a century egg because he's well preserved and durable.

While Loud and Louder were debating the qualities of a century egg, Smooth Voice sent me a WhatsApp message ordering me to order Loud and Louder to go to a song immediately.

We had to drop the comparison between foods and world leaders.

After the show, the three of us were called into Smooth Voice's office. He looked flustered. He explained to the giggly DJs that he had been fielding calls all morning about the Prime Minister and century eggs. The comparison had not gone down well. Mr Loud pointed out that the century egg reference was entirely complimentary. The century egg represented longevity and good health.

'The century egg is a funny shape,' said Smooth Voice. 'You're comparing him to a squidgy food. They don't want any more comparisons to foods.'

'But we'd been doing it all morning,' said Mr Louder. 'We compared Trump to an orange.'

'Well, that's different,' said Smooth Voice. 'He *is* orange.'

Mr Louder leaned forward and said, 'And our Prime Minister is not actually a century egg?'

'You know what I mean. You went too far,' said Smooth Voice. 'There were complaints about the century egg. They said you were being disrespectful.'

Mr Loud reiterated that we had called the British Prime Minister a lettuce and the Australian Prime Minister a banana. Smooth Voice insisted that those foods were different. They were playful, funny foods.

The egg was not a funny food.

Smooth Voice said, 'It's like you're calling him an "egg head".'

Mr Loud reminded him that egg heads were clever.

Smooth Voice said, 'Yeah, but when you think of egg heads, you think of Dr Evil.'

Loud and Louder had to promise not to compare the Prime Minister with unfunny foods in future, especially eggs.

The Prime Minister was not an unfunny food.

The Prime Minister was not an egghead.

The Prime Minister was not Dr Evil.

We had to be clear on that.

Day 75

Mr Louder arrived with a hangover and a hoarse voice this morning. He refused to record another 'cheesy advertorial' so he asked me to do it instead. According to Mr Louder, the marketing department had already cleared the text and wouldn't care who read out the 'diarrhoea as long as it dribbled over the airwaves'. I was reluctant. We had already received a warning about prime ministers and century eggs. But Mr Louder said, 'Darling, it wouldn't matter if I died of a heart attack after having sex under the desk, as long as the advertorial went out. Believe me, they won't care.'

I pulled the mic towards me as I pictured Mr Louder having sex under the desk. After a deep breath, I recorded the following advertorial:

> 'This property segment was brought to you by the Le Rainforest, a freehold condo development in Bukit Timah, bringing the luxurious tranquillity of green living to every home. Love Nature? Then live here.'

Mr Louder complimented me on my sexy delivery.

'Sounds like a nice place,' I said, changing the subject.

Mr Louder sipped his black coffee and said, 'It should be. They chopped down the rainforest to build it.'

Day 76

Smooth Voice popped into the studio for a quick chat this morning. He had received a complaint from the marketing department. Apparently, a slow, sultry female voice made the prestigious Le Rainforest sound like a massage parlour advertising a 'special service'.

Slow, sultry female voices do not sell $5 million condo units in Singapore. Only Mr Louder's slightly effeminate voice sold $5 million condo units in Singapore. I tried to push back on the blatant sexism. Smooth Voice took my objections on board but informed me that the client had a longstanding relationship with the radio station.

He did offer some professional advice though. He suggested that I speed up my delivery and speak in a slightly higher pitch.

'So I won't sound like I'm selling sex,' I said. 'I'll sound like I'm actually having sex.'

'That might help with our Nielsen ratings,' said Mr Louder.

Smooth Voice didn't appreciate the sarcasm. He said, 'Hey, I'm being serious here. They've got a long-term contract with us. Please. Just get it done.' Smooth Voice's abrupt tone shocked me. He was usually an easy-going guy.

Mr Loud was not impressed. He said, 'What did you mention the Nielsen ratings for?'

Mr Louder shrugged it off as a joke.

But the ratings were not a joke for Mr Loud. The next ratings survey was being conducted in a month or so. Mr Loud didn't get as many corporate gigs as Mr Louder.

Later, we received a copy of the client's email, which made the following requests.

The voice for the Le Rainforest development was not to sound sexy or sleazy.

The voice for the Le Rainforest development was to sound authoritative.

The voice for the Le Rainforest development had to appeal to leading businessmen.

'Well, I do find leading businessmen appealing,' said Mr Louder. The DJ found the irony hysterical and promised to put on his most 'butch' voice.

Luckily, my sleazy voice was still allowed to record the weather, which was easy. It's always sunny in Singapore, right?

Day 77

I was eating kaya toast for breakfast when I realised that the client's demands for *'the voice of the Le Rainforest development'* were essentially saying '*the*' twice.

In the afternoon, I noticed that our online advertorial for Le Rainforest condo project had also included the redundant '*the*' in the text.

Trying to help – and kiss ass a little bit – I sent a WhatsApp message to Mother Superior.

I wrote, 'Hello, Mother Superior. Hope you are well. It's Millie Lee here. Sorry to bother you, but that condo advertorial in the Singapore section has "the" and "le" beside each other. I know you don't like juxtaposition. Ha ha!'

She sent me a four-word reply in block caps.

'SINGAPOREANS DON'T SPEAK FRENCH!'

Day 80

There was a big radio meeting today. All the major bosses attended. Even Slick Scholar showed up. He sat beside me, asked how I was doing and didn't touch, squeeze or rub any of my body parts, which was a refreshing change. Smooth Voice looked even more agitated than usual. His yellow fingers kept tapping the table. There were rumours of another retrenchment exercise and this meeting ensured he was going to be at least half an hour from his next smoke break. Captain Mayhem sat at the head of the table. He looked ready for an afternoon snooze. He did compliment me on my weather reports, which he always watched on our live YouTube channel. He asked if I had considered using a ring light in the studio.

Loud and Louder scrolled through their phones. They had a lunchtime gig with a local bank, which paid them more than a week's worth of breakfast shows. For them, the radio work was a means to an end. The primetime breakfast slot put them in the shop window for more lucrative corporate events.

On the news side, the journalists hoped for a dramatic scoop.

On the radio side, the DJs hoped to sell a new banking app at a Raffles Place roadshow.

I'd rather quit than prostrate myself in that way.

Smooth Voice cleared his throat. There was a lot of phlegm to clear. He was eager to start. He was eager to get to his next smoke break.

'We've all read the news online,' he said. 'Other radio stations have laid off staff, restructured, rebranded and so on. We're not immune to that either.'

Loud and Louder stopped scrolling through their phones. Their profile would sustain their corporate gigs for a while, but every artiste has a shelf life in Singapore. They still needed the Rojak Breakfast Show, no matter how much they might pretend otherwise.

'So what's happening to our show?'

Mr Loud sounded a bit desperate, which was understandable. He was older and less marketable. Unlike Mr Louder, he only appealed to one demographic.

'The show is fine,' said Smooth Voice. 'We're working with Sales Guru on branding and sponsorship opportunities, which is why your upcoming roadshow is critical.'

The upcoming roadshow had been months in the planning.

The upcoming roadshow was being held at Velocity @ Novena, a shopping mall with a stupid symbol in its name to show how hip it was with the right crowd.

The upcoming roadshow was a chance to find a new, younger audience.

To do that, the upcoming roadshow was going to launch a Durian Frappuccino.

Smooth Voice reminded us that Sales Guru had secured a prime slot for us, right outside the coffee franchise that expected to sell hundreds of Durian Frappuccinos on launch day.

Captain Mayhem took over the meeting. He said, 'In branding terms, this is going to be the biggest event for your show since the pandemic. It's a multi-pronged marketing event, with ads being placed online and on our TV channels, too. It's going to show the best of us to a huge crowd.'

The men in the meeting then decided that I would attend the roadshow dressed as a durian.

Day 87

After a week of frantic planning, Sales Guru briefed me today on my responsibilities at tomorrow's roadshow.

I wasn't going to be dressed as a random durian anymore.

I was going to be dressed as the official durian.

This was a big deal for the client. I was wearing the licensed costume of a character that was going to appear on the side of every Durian Frappuccino cup. My character did not yet boast a name. The client couldn't decide between 'Duri' and 'Frappy', so they had opted to give my character an air of mystery: The Durian With No Name.

Besides, the track record of durian-flavoured products wasn't great, according to Sales Guru, and the client was being cautious ahead of the launch. Apparently, a durian chocolate bar, a durian ice-cream, a durian pie and durian instant coffees had all been marketed previously. Most had flopped.

But the Durian Frappuccino had tested well with Gen Z – my people, according to Sales Guru, who was three whole years older than me – and the client had liked the idea of me wearing the costume.

'It helps that you're, you know,' said Sales Guru, pointing at my face.

I felt so honoured.

'And people will see your face, which is good, so try not to sweat too much,' she added.

I promised not to sweat too much in a life-sized durian costume.

Sales Guru went through a list of the client's recommendations on her iPad.

As the official durian, I was not to use inappropriate language in front of the crowd, especially children.

As the official durian, I was not to be photographed with anything inappropriate.

'Like what?' I wondered. 'A paedophile?'

Sales Guru blushed and said, 'No *lah*, I think the client means rival products, like different coffee brands. And you cannot smoke inside the costume.'

'Even if I catch fire?'

Sales Guru ignored me. She took the client's list of recommendations on her iPad very seriously. She said, 'This is a bit embarrassing, but they wanted me to mention it at least. No offensive smells.'

I was incredulous.

She said, 'Yeah, they say that durians have a bad stereotype when it comes to smells. So our durian cannot smell bad at the roadshow. Just wear nice perfume *lah*.'

Day 88

I made media history today. I read the hourly weather reports in a durian costume.

In fact, I read the hourly weather reports in a durian costume outside Velocity @ Novena, during the busy rush-hour crowd, in front of commuters, shoppers, staff from the nearby Tan Tock Seng Hospital, two old NTU classmates who happened to be passing through and a bratty child who kept poking me in the stomach to see if I was real.

I proved that I was real by stepping on the little bugger's toes.

His crying almost interrupted *the song*.

The new Durian Frappuccino came with a song.

According to Sales Guru, market research showed that simple, repetitive lyrics worked best, because Singaporeans were still in kindergarten.

Loud and Louder played the following ditty at regular intervals.

If you like coffee, coffee, coffee, coffee, coffee,
And you like durian, durian, durian, durian, durian,
Then mixy, mixy, mixy, mixy, mixy,
And dabao *a Durian Frappuccino today.*

It didn't make sense. It didn't even scan. But it didn't matter because there was a dance.

There was a dance for the official Durian Frappuccino, which was me.

On the first line, I had to pretend to slurp from a cup.

On the second line, I had to shake my durian scales.

On the third line, I had to wiggle my durian ass.

On the fourth line, I had to hand out discount vouchers.

At the end of the song, I had to stop little kids from hugging my crotch.

The roadshow was three hours long and Loud and Louder were obligated to play the song three times an hour.

I was obligated to drop everything and dance whenever Loud and Louder played the song.

They played the song six times in the first hour alone.

In the second hour, they deliberately hit the jingle straight after the weather report, so I said, 'It's going to be sunny, with a chance of rain in the afternoon and a top temperature of thirty-two degrees ... *If you like coffee, coffee, coffee, coffee, coffee ...*'

Bastards.

By the third hour, I had kids running up to me, wiggling their asses and demanding that I sing the 'funny mixy, mixy song'. I pointed out that the song could only be played at regular intervals. But Mr Louder overheard the conversation and insisted that we had to give the fans what they wanted.

The song was played eight times in the final hour.

Sweat poured down my face. My underwear was drenched, and a nervous Sales Guru wondered aloud if I was 'conveying a positive image for the product'. I told her that my knickers were soaking wet and I didn't care about the product's image.

Sales Guru sympathised. She handed me a single sheet from her tissue packet, which was like giving me Scotch tape on the Titanic.

I was dragging the tissue across my red face when my parents turned up to 'support me'.

My father supported me by asking if I got paid extra for being dressed as a durian.

My mother supported me by saying the Durian Frappuccino costume made me look fat.

Then they asked me to take a photo of them with Loud and Louder. My mother asked Mr Louder why he was wearing so much make-up. My father asked Mr Loud how much money he made.

They didn't want a photo with me, of course. I was an underpaid, fat durian. But the roadshow had otherwise been a success. The client was happy with their Durian Frappuccino sales. Sales Guru was happy that the client was happy. And Loud and Louder were happy that Sales Guru was happy that the client was happy because the client booked them for lucrative hosting gigs.

No one seemed to mention the actual radio show.

We were almost ready to pack up, with fifteen minutes to go, when Loud and Louder reminded the crowd at Velocity @ Novena that there was a music contest coming up, with a prize of $1000.

And that's when the nightmare really began.

I had forgotten about the music contest. I had also forgotten that it was my job to pick a contestant from the crowd. Loud and Louder had already briefed me.

Keep away from the competition addicts, they had said repeatedly.

The competition addicts called into the Rojak Breakfast Show regularly. They turned up at the roadshows. They took part in every competition, no matter how crappy the prize.

And most of our prizes were crappy.

We gave away golf umbrellas. These guys didn't play golf and still wanted them.

We gave away car decal stickers and most of the callers didn't own a car.

There was a longstanding theory that some of the participants were lonely and just enjoyed a friendly, familiar voice at the end of the line, which might be true if they didn't go nuts if their car decal stickers didn't show up.

And today was going to be even worse. We were not giving away car decal stickers or umbrellas or mugs, T-shirts, keyrings and all the other branded stuff that a marketing executive had once decided should have the Rojak Breakfast Show logo splashed all over it.

We were giving away a prize of $1000, thanks to the folks behind the Durian Frappuccino. And the human Durian Frappuccino – me – had to filter out the suspected competition addicts from the genuinely random radio fans. I settled on a Chinese retiree. He was relatively smart, wearing chino shorts and a polo shirt from that shop that all the uncles like. His English was good enough and he had a cheeky persona. Without saying a word, I gestured towards Loud and Louder. The DJs nodded their approval.

I pulled him out of the crowd. He introduced himself as Sam from Whampoa.

Loud and Louder played the competition jingle. The shopping

mall fell mostly silent. The competition was on.

Loud and Louder played five short clips, no more than a couple of seconds each and Sam from Whampoa had to correctly guess the names of both the song and the artist.

He was amazing.

Maybe he was a competition addict after all, but Loud and Louder didn't recognise him and didn't care. He was a natural: chirpy and giggly. He made the crowd laugh with his jovial answers, reeling them off in quick succession.

Number one: 'Take on Me' by A-Ha.

Number two: 'We Will Rock You' by Queen.

Number three: 'Words' by The Bee Gees.

Number four: 'Close to You' by The Carpenters

The first four were the standard playlist on most Singaporean radio stations, a weird combination of pop classics, soft rock and ballads.

The fifth and final song was also a ballad, but a lesser-known ballad from the 1960s. But Sam from Whampoa's eyes lit up immediately. He grabbed the mic I was holding. His hand was now covering mine.

I had the sweatier hand, but then I was the one dressed as a durian.

Sam from Whampoa said, 'It's "Please Release Me"!'

His voice boomed across the Novena shopping mall. He was going to do this. He was going to win $1000.

'And the artist?' My voice was almost as loud as his. I was just as excited. We all were.

Even my mother had her hands clasped, looking like she was about to pray.

He said, 'Er, let me think ah.'

Sam from Whampoa hesitated. Sam from Whampoa wasn't sure. Sam from Whampoa was crushing my fingers against the mic.

Loud and Louder played the sound of a ticking clock, which made the tension unbearable. I noticed the staff in Burger King had even stopped serving to watch. The sweat trickled through our intertwined fingers. 'Not much time left, Sam,' I whispered.

'Wait ah, wait ah.' Sam from Whampoa raised his index finger into the air, like he was checking the wind direction.

'I got it, I got it,' he shouted, dragging the mic to his lips. 'It's Angle Berk Humping Dick!'

The crowd were already giggling. I had no idea who sang the song. I didn't have the answers, but I was pretty sure it wasn't Angle Berk Humping Dick. But the older people in the crowd were already clapping. I looked over at Loud and Louder for guidance. They had the jingles, one for winning, one for losing. But they hadn't played either. I noticed Mr Loud's fingers hovering over the radio panel. He switched on his mic. He said, 'Let's hear that answer one more time.'

Sam from Whampoa said, 'Angle Berk Humping Dick! Angle Berk Humping Dick!'

The more he said it, the sillier it sounded. Surely, there was no singer called Angle Berk Humping Dick. I would've known if there was a singer called Angle Berk Humping Dick.

Now Mr Loud turned to Mr Louder for guidance. Mr Louder looked out at the crowd. The younger ones were laughing. The older ones were applauding. Mr Louder shrugged and hit a button. 'It's the correct answer,' he said.

Sam from Whampoa hugged me. 'I knew it. Angle Berk Humping Dick,' he cried.

After the show, Sam from Whampoa was presented with one of those large, fake publicity cheques for $1000. I had to present it to him, being the official Durian Frappuccino. Loud and Louder flanked us for the photographs.

'We're gonna get shit for this,' said Mr Louder, through gritted teeth, as he waved at the crowd.

'Yeah, I can't believe there's a singer called Humping Dick,' I said. 'Will we get fined for saying that on air?'

'Don't know,' said Mr Louder. 'The singer's name is Engelbert Humperdinck.'

I assumed we'd be OK then.

'No, we won't,' said Mr Louder, still waving to the crowd. 'And you stink in that costume.'

Day 89

I went viral today. I went viral dressed as a Durian Frappuccino.

First, the Instagrammers came for me. But I did nothing because I was not allowed to comment on Instagram in a professional capacity.

Then the independent news sites came for me. But I ignored their emails because I did not work for the independent news sites.

And then rival radio stations came for me. But it didn't matter what I did by then as the story was everywhere. There was nothing I could do to stop the public humiliation.

My best friend from school called and requested a song by Angle Berk Humping Dick.

My mother reminded me that I'd never get a husband if I dressed like a durian.

And my father stayed in his bedroom to search 'Angle Berk Humping Dick' on Google.

Loud and Louder and I got through the breakfast show by not making any reference to the roadshow competition or the mispronunciation of Engelbert Humperdinck in the feeble hope that the storm in a Durian Frappuccino cup might blow over.

No chance.

We were being torn to shreds online.

We were being accused of Chinese privilege, racial privilege, uncle privilege, sponsor privilege and all other sorts of bias and prejudices. No one was spared. Poor Sam from Whampoa was being mocked for his mispronunciation. Loud and Louder were being ridiculed for their lack of professionalism.

The radio station was being accused of corruption.

And I was being labelled the ugliest durian of all time, which must be a seriously competitive field.

During the breakfast show, I was instructed to ignore all the social media comments about durians, mispronunciations and dodgy competitions and focus only on the other comments.

But there weren't any other comments.

Instead, we had seventeen requests for any songs by Angle Berk Humping Dick. One smart ass suggested that we call ourselves 'The Angle, Berk and Humping Dick' show.

Surprisingly, Mr Louder didn't mind the idea of being known as Humping Dick.

Not surprisingly, Mr Loud was less keen to be known as a berk.

But I had a greater concern. I was barely four months into my media probationary period, and I was already stuck with an unwanted association. Random searches for smelly fruits or humping dicks were likely to throw up photos of me, dressed as the ugliest durian of all time, apparently.

By 10am, someone had registered the domain name of angleberkhumpingdick.com.

By lunchtime, Lazada and Shoppee were already selling T-shirts with 'Angle Berk Humping Dick' across the front.

At 1pm, an emergency meeting was convened in Captain Mayhem's office. The atmosphere was funereal. We might as well have gone in wearing black armbands. Captain Mayhem didn't even bother with his transparent uncle flirting. He barely looked up at me, preferring to stare at his laptop.

Sales Guru sat at the side of his desk. She looked like she might burst into tears at any moment. Smooth Voice sat alongside her, scrolling through his phone for updates.

Standing up against the glass wall, Slick Scholar offered a sympathetic smile, which didn't help. His lean frame made him even more crushingly handsome than usual. But I was in no mood to feel that way, not today.

Luckily, Hokkien Half-Ball was also present to sustain my shitty frame of mind. I asked why he was in the room. My tone was abrupt. I was obviously irritated, but I didn't care. I was being punished for the sins of everyone else in the room.

Captain Mayhem and Smooth Voice had wanted silly public gimmicks in a cynical attempt to attract a younger audience.

Sales Guru had approved the ridiculous costume to pacify her demanding client.

Loud and Louder had lacked the balls to challenge the pronunciation.

Sam from Whampoa couldn't say the name properly and Hokkien Half-Ball was an asshole.

And Slick Scholar oversaw all of them.

But none of their faces popped up in my father's 'humping dick' searches. Only mine did.

Hokkien Half-Ball was standing beside Slick Scholar, but visibly shrinking. He said, 'I'm the lifestyle editor, Millie. It's a lifestyle story.'

'It's a bloody nightmare,' said Captain Mayhem, closing his laptop. 'The BBC has just picked it up. Apparently, they are seeking a response from Engelbert Humperdinck's representatives.'

'Wah, he's still alive,' said Mr Louder.

'Yes, he's still alive,' said Captain Mayhem. 'But this might bloody kill him.'

Smooth Voice coughed to express his embarrassment or clear his nicotine-coated phlegm. It was hard to tell.

He said, 'The competition didn't really hurt us though. The social media numbers are really strong and still rising. It's getting a lot of traction on YouTube and TikTok, which are our target audiences.'

'That's because they're searching for swinging dicks,' said Captain Mayhem.

'It's, er, humping dick,' said Mr Louder. 'They're looking for humping dicks.'

'Oh, now you correct someone's speech,' said Captain Mayhem. 'Why didn't you correct his speech yesterday? Why didn't you say his answer was incorrect yesterday?'

'We didn't want to offend him,' said Mr Loud.

Captain Mayhem stared at the two DJs. He was only a few years older but seemed generations away. He said, 'Wait ah. He says humping dick on national radio and you're worried about offending *him*?'

'Pronunciation is a sensitive issue in Singapore. It's happened so many times before,' said Smooth Voice, between coughing fits.

'Then why have these competitions if they're so troublesome?' said Captain Mayhem.

Sales Guru had this one covered. 'Our clients like it. They like the prize component, brings in the crowd, positive publicity.'

'This is not positive publicity,' said Captain Mayhem. He looked like a melting candle.

Sales Guru said, 'Actually, I put together a quick slide presentation on that.'

Sales Guru opened her laptop.

Sales Guru began fumbling for an HDMI cable.

Sales Guru was going to conduct an impromptu slide presentation.

Sales Guru could not read the room.

Everyone else just stared at her.

Slick Scholar said, 'I don't think we need a slide presentation now.'

Sales Guru said, 'It's just a quick one, showing hits and clicks across a twelve-hour period.'

She found the HDMI cable slot. 'It'll show the positive impact of the campaign,' she added.

'Maybe later,' suggested Smooth Voice.

'Understand. But the client is privately pleased with the expanding coverage. Brand awareness has gone through the roof,' said Sales Guru, clicking her keyboard.

I said, 'Please. I don't wanna see any more photos of me dressed like a durian.'

My unexpected outburst ended Sales Guru's slide presentation.

Captain Mayhem moved his laptop to the side. 'Well, we know how Millie feels about this.'

'Sorry,' I muttered. 'But this is not fair on me, or my parents. My mother has been crying about all the online content.'

She hadn't. But I sensed the sympathy from everyone at the meeting, except from Sales Guru. She looked ready to slice my throat with her laptop.

'Millie is right,' said Slick Scholar. 'It was an unfortunate confluence of events. Mispronunciations and racial and cultural sensitivities brought us to this point. I'm not entirely sure what else the boys could've done in that awkward situation.'

The boys were Loud and Louder. They were at least a decade older than Slick Scholar.

'Exactly,' said Mr Louder. 'If we don't give him the prize, we are accused of being insensitive, suggesting his English is not so powerful. If we do give him the prize, we get accused of favouring the Chinese and our rival stations whack us. We can't win.'

'But Sam from Whampoa did and we'll just have to suck it up,' said Slick Scholar. 'Take what's coming our way for the next couple of days. And Millie, if I were you, maybe stay off social media for a bit. This shit will blow over by tomorrow.'

Day 90

A famous social media influencer dropped a video of him wearing an Angle Berk Humping Dick T-Shirt and singing Engelbert Humperdinck's' *Please Release* Me.

In the afternoon, the Goethe-Institut Singapore sent out the following marketing email.

Are German names tough? Come and learn the right way at the Goethe-Institut. Please. Release the German in you!

In the evening, a low-cost airline published an ad campaign for cheap Australian flights. The headline?

Please release me to Perth.

I'm so glad this shit has blown over.

Day 93

We were called into Smooth Voice's office after the breakfast show. Our station director wanted to share the latest directive from upstairs.

There will be no more radio competitions that involve pronunciation. Loud and Louder thought it was a joke. Smooth Voice reassured them that it was not.

'But we're a radio show,' said Mr Loud. 'How can competitions not involve speech?'

Smooth Voice fiddled with his lighter. 'I didn't say speech. I said pronunciation.'

Mr Louder wondered if there was a difference.

Smooth Voice said, 'Yeah, the difference is, they didn't say speech, they just said pronunciation. Any prizes cannot involve pronunciation, OK? Just use texts or something?'

Mr Louder said, 'Can we do contests with sign language?'

Smooth Voice said, 'Just do this for me. Oh, and I've removed Engelbert Humperdinck from the playlist. Just in case.'

'Just in case what? It's 1967 again? We don't play Engelbert Humperdinck,' said Mr Loud.

Smooth Voice told us not to shoot the messenger. He was just relaying the bosses' messages. No music from Humperdinck. No more quizzes involving pronunciation.

Mr Louder pointed at me and said, 'But she can still dress like a durian, right?'

I threw a pen at him. I was going to miss these guys.

Day 96

I met Lauren at a bar tonight. She was in a giddy mood. Her

arts and literature articles had impressed the editors. Her byline was appearing almost daily and there were rumours of a possible promotion.

Strangely, I couldn't remember my last byline and I wasn't particularly bothered. I had gone viral as a durian though and Lauren loved the radio gossip. 'What's the latest?' She asked, sipping her prosecco.

'It's died down a bit now,' I said, truthfully.

'Was there any action taken?'

'What for? We gave the guy the money. It's not like we made fun of him. Everyone else made fun of him. And me.'

'Yeah, I saw the durian memes.'

So had my parents. My mother had cancelled her weekly mahjong game again.

Lauren also filled me in on the gossip from the newsroom. Apparently, more journalists were being 'asked to leave the company', which was a nice way of firing them, to save face, cut costs and build a dynamic media company for the 21st century.

The dynamic editors doing the firing were around my father's age. They kept their jobs to create content that would appeal to readers around my age, which made perfect sense.

Lauren had been tasked with 'ramping up digital audio content to enhance the consumer experience.'

In other words, she had to make a podcast.

'You could come on if you want, as the viral durian,' she said.

I told her what she could do with her podcast.

'Hey, I'm not making a podcast,' she said. 'I'm producing digital audio content to enhance the consumer experience. A viral durian could push up my numbers.'

I also told her where she could push her numbers.

I said, 'The durian thing is dead now. People have moved on already.'

On the MRT ride home, a mother asked if her little boy could take a selfie with the 'dancing durian'.

Day 100

Smooth Voice is also thinking about a new podcast for Loud and Louder, AKA additional digital audio content to enhance the consumer experience. To gauge interest, he asked me to compile a list of the most popular topics from today's show, based on our listeners' comments and texts.

I came up with the following top five:

At five, there was BTO apartment sales.
At four, there was the spike in Covid-19 cases.
At three, there was the Jay Chou concert.
At two, there was a new burger at McDonalds.
At one, there was the monkey in the mirror.

The monkey wasn't actually in a mirror. A construction worker at the Mandai Animal Paradise construction site took a video of a long-tailed macaque that appeared to be mimicking human actions.

It wasn't. The construction worker was copying the monkey's actions. According to one commentator below the Instagram clip, it was the funniest thing he'd ever seen.

And Singapore produced the *Ah Boys to Men* movies.

It's like we've got too much good comedy in this country.

Day 101

Smooth Voice called me into his office today. The monkey in the mirror was still trending. And its habitat was being developed by the Singapore Wildlife Sanctuary Group, which was one of our biggest advertisers and eager to improve its corporate image.

So, I was sent to the Mandai forest.

My job was to find the monkey in the mirror.

My second job was to interview the monkey in the mirror.

Not in a serious way – because that would be silly – but in a quirky, tongue-in-cheek way, at a safe distance, and on my phone.

Smooth Voice thought a light-hearted video would work well on our social media channels. We needed to boost our Instagram reel numbers and rehabilitate the show's reputation, after the Humperdinck debacle.

Naturally, the best way to bounce back after playing a dancing durian in a shopping mall was to conduct a video interview with a monkey in the forest. But I wasn't Jane Goodall. I struggled to recognise myself when I woke up in the morning. How was I going to find and recognise a monkey from a shaky Instagram clip?

Fortunately, the forest and the monkey population had both shrunk considerably, which made my job a bit easier.

At dusk, I met my old friends from the Singapore Wildlife Sanctuary Group. The director of the corporate communications division, sustainability and conservation, greeted me at the boardwalk entrance of their unfinished eco-tourism development. The deputy director stood just behind the director. And the young executive stood behind the deputy director, clutching a clipboard filled with bullet points.

'It's good to see you again, Miss Lee,' said the director.

'Yes, good to see you again,' said the deputy director.

'Here's our latest information pack,' said the young executive, passing me a heavy folder filled with papers.

I wondered why they had put together an information pack on the monkey in the mirror.

She turned bright red and said, 'No this is an updated list of our conservation initiatives.'

And with that, we set off in search of a needle in a haystack.

After an hour, I'd seen dozens of sleepy, sweaty construction workers, too many toppled trees, some cranes and piles of scaffolding.

The young executive had offered to provide me with several 'humorous' story angles for my monkey in the mirror video, which all seemed to involve interviewing the CEO of the Singapore Wildlife Sanctuary Group.

The director had offered to give me a private media tour of the development once it was completed.

And the deputy director had privately offered me dinner on Thursday night.

I was close to accepting all three offers, just to escape the hot air (only half of it came from the forest.)

In fact, I was ready to call it a day when I heard a rustling up ahead. A long-tailed macaque was sitting on the boardwalk, eating some fruits. I wasn't sure if it was the monkey in the mirror.

I didn't care if it was the monkey in the mirror.

I was interviewing that monkey.

I quietly took out my phone, zoomed in on my interview subject, hit record and said: 'So, er ... Monkey. I'm Millie Lee, a reporter. Are you the famous monkey in the mirror?'

The monkey scratched its testicles.

I said, 'Ah, that must be a "yes" then. So what's it like being the most famous primate since Ah Meng?'

The monkey scratched its testicles again.

I said, 'Yes, I bet the sudden fame is quite stressful, right?'

When I heard the stifled giggling among the employees of the Singapore Wildlife Sanctuary Group, I thought I might be onto something.

Day 103

My monkey video interview was ridiculed for three hours on our Rojak Breakfast Show this morning.

My monkey video interview was the most watched clip across all our platforms, even though we had a special on the Israel crisis.

After the show, Captain Mayhem asked to see me in his office.

When I went in, he was looking at his laptop, giggling.

'Your video is so funny,' he said. 'I watch it over and over, the part where he scratches himself. Damn funny.'

'Most of the credit goes to the producers,' I replied, honestly.

They had edited the clips to make the monkey's movements mirror my own. At times, he did look like he was genuinely responding to my questions. If he 'answered' favourably, he fiddled with his testicles. If he disagreed, he either shook his head or showed his ass.

Mostly, he fiddled with his testicles. Mostly, Captain Mayhem laughed at the testicle-fiddling. 'Ah, so good,' he said, closing his laptop.

'Thank you.'

'There is something about you that is different,' said Captain Mayhem, peering down at my chest.

I asked how I was different.

He said, 'You see things from an unusual angle. Look what you did with this video.'

'It was actually Smooth Voice's idea,' I pointed out.

'Actually, it was mine,' said Captain Mayhem, moving his focus towards my legs. 'I felt the guys at the Sanctuary Group needed better coverage.'

I had to point out that the so-called better coverage was a video of a monkey scratching its genitals.

Captain Mayhem sat up and said, 'No, it's a distraction, for them and us. We've got the latest Nielsen Ratings survey coming up. We need these eyeballs. That's why I want you and the guys to interview the Female Minister.'

'Because I interviewed a monkey?'

Captain Mayhem laughed loudly and then pointed at me. 'No, because of that,' he said.

He was pointing at my breasts. I looked down at my breasts,

feeling confused.

'Your irreverent tone,' he added quickly. 'You know the Female Minister right? She's got a reputation for being stiff. Too straight. She wants to change that before the election, so I've suggested an interview with Loud and Louder, with you sitting in. Did you know she shared your monkey video on Facebook?'

I had no idea. I had no idea what to do with that information either. Media movies like *Spotlight* made me want to be a journalist. There were no media movies about female ministers sharing videos of a monkey scratching its nuts.

I knew that interviewing a government minister was a huge opportunity. Slick Scholar usually organised and conducted these assignments with a handpicked team. They needed to be handled with care. And I was still on probation.

I had to be honest. I said, 'I'm not sure I'd be right for this, especially on our show. The tone might be different from her typical interviews.'

'That's exactly what she wants,' said Captain Mayhem. 'Something less serious and more personal. She knows she's seen as too scripted.'

I suggested that I wouldn't know what to say to the Female Minister off the cuff.

He said, 'Ah, it's OK. We'll give you a script to follow.'

Day 105

Captain Mayhem called a meeting with The Rojak Breakfast

crew, Smooth Voice and Slick Scholar to discuss the upcoming interview with the Female Minister.

Our CEO wanted to emphasise the delicate balancing act between showing the Female Minister's lighter side on a playful media format, whilst recognising that a ministerial interview might be the kiss of death in ratings terms, especially among younger listeners.

Our rivals had recently reported a significant jump in listenership and this interview really could go either way – for ourselves and the Female Minister.

No pressure then.

Captain Mayhem looked around the mahogany table for fresh ideas.

He said, 'The Female Minister wants the chat to feel natural and spontaneous. So we need to be prepared and well-rehearsed so the chat feels natural and spontaneous.'

Mr Loud suggested the Female Minister pick her favourite songs to play.

Slick Scholar wasn't keen. Apparently, a minister had once picked Elton John as his favourite artist, which was seen in some quarters as endorsing an alternative lifestyle.

Mr Louder suggested the Female Minister perform *YMCA* for the in-studio camera.

Slick Scholar ignored him.

Smooth Voice suggested a 'guess the next lyric' game with the Female Minister, to show that she was across popular culture.

Slick Scholar pointed out that all lyrics would need to be cleared in advance, which might defeat the purpose of the game.

I suggested making the Female Minister a DJ for a day,

allowing her to read out the news and weather.

Slick Scholar liked the idea but pointed out that the news and weather would have to be cleared in advance. Even our government can't prepare the weather in advance.

Captain Mayhem reiterated his eagerness to have the Female Minster interact with the public in a way that came across as fun and natural, even though it was contrived and manufactured.

Mr Louder suggested we bring in the monkey.

After half an hour of increasingly bitchy squabbling, Captain Mayhem insisted that he was open to anything other than a straight interview.

After an hour of very bitchy squabbling, we agreed on a straight interview with a humorous twist. I would ask the Female Minister for her thoughts on my monkey video.

Day 107

Spent the day writing questions that sounded conversational and off-the-cuff.

Spent the evening rewriting questions that sounded conversational and off-the-cuff.

Spent the night rehearsing the approved questions sent to me by Slick Scholar, with the instruction that they sounded conversational and off-the-cuff.

Day 109

Spent the day rewriting the approved questions, following feedback from the Female Minister's office.

Spent the evening incorporating answers provided by the Female Minister's office into a dummy script.

Spent the night reassuring the Female Minister's office that the final list of approved questions and approved answers would still sound conversational and off-the-cuff.

Day 112

After the Rojak Breakfast Show, Loud and Louder and I stayed back in the studio to rehearse tomorrow's interview.

Loud and Louder played themselves. I played the Female Minister. Slick Scholar played a representative from the Female Minister's office, standing at the back of the cramped radio studio and taking notes.

He recommended softer lighting for the actual interview as 'not everyone looks like Millie, do they?'

Loud and Louder found his comment hilarious because he was their boss. I was supposed to find his comment insulting. But his smile made me think of Henry Golding in that Christmas romcom instead.

Secretly, I liked the compliment.

Slick Scholar then said, 'We have to accept that the Female

Minister won't sound as relaxed as Millie either. That's the elephant in the room.'

Mr Louder said, 'We'd be better off with that monkey in the room.'

Day 113

The most important day of my new career began drenched in sweat. I had the worst dream.

Our radio studio was deep inside the forest. Loud and Louder were dressed as staff members of the Singapore Wildlife Sanctuary Group. They read their questions from clipboards.

We were playing '*Name that Tune*' with the Female Minister, but she insisted that every tune was *YMCA* and broke out her *YMCA* moves.

My job was to copy her moves whilst eating rambutan fruits. Whenever my mimicry impressed Loud and Louder, they hit a red button and an 'applause' sign lit up. The audience jumped up and down, clapping wildly.

They were all monkeys.

Captain Mayhem kept popping up above a tree stump like a Whac-A-Mole character, shouting 'natural and spontaneous, natural and spontaneous'. He wouldn't stop until Mr Louder whacked him over the head with a clipboard.

The dream only ended when my mother shook me awake. She reminded me that all her mahjong friends would be watching the interview on YouTube and I shouldn't wear anything fattening.

We got through the first hour of the Rojak Breakfast Show on autopilot. Even Mr Louder was unusually subdued. He was the flamboyant extrovert but was clearly censoring himself. After a news report about an extreme weather event in the United States, he made a lame joke about uncontrolled wind in the Deep South, but it was all a bit half-hearted.

And then the Female Minister arrived during a song break.

First, a buff security guy with an earpiece came in and wandered around the studio. He looked under my chair and noticed an unusual object poking through the side of my bag.

It was my banana.

He stared at it briefly, before deciding that I wasn't likely to give the Female Minister a lethal dose of potassium.

Second, the executive of something or other from the Female Minister's office hurried in, clutching the pre-approved questions and answers on several stapled pieces of A4 and politely reminded us to stick to the script.

Mr Louder thought about responding, but Slick Scholar's eyes shut him down. Our national editor stood at the back of the studio, arms folded, just observing.

And finally, Captain Mayhem ushered Female Minister into the studio, as if she were a frail auntie. He introduced us one at a time.

'This is Loud and Louder, the hosts of our flagship breakfast show,' the CEO gushed.

'Yes, I've been listening to the show for many years,' said Female Minister.

'But I've only been hosting the show for eight months,' said Mr Louder.

Female Minister looked embarrassed. Slick Scholar looked horrified. Captain Mayhem looked like he was passing a kidney stone.

The executive of something or other from the Female Minister's office looked through the pre-approved questions and answers. Mr Louder had gone off-script and the interview hadn't even started yet.

Female Minister stared at Mr Louder. Everyone else in the cramped, claustrophobic studio stared at Female Minister. No one dared to speak before she did.

Finally, she said, 'And that's why I've been listening to the show for many years. For your quick wit.'

And Mr Louder said, 'Eh, not bad, ah, this one.'

Within seconds, the air was filled with fake laughter.

We were going to be fine after that.

The interview went on longer than expected, mostly because the Female Minister kept going off-script. She was a genuinely remarkable woman: smart, articulate and an unbelievably quick thinker. Ironically, she only sounded superficial when she followed the pre-approved answers. When she went off on a tangent, I found myself a captive audience.

She was fascinating, so much so, that I missed my cue.

According to the pre-approved flow of the interview, I was supposed to come in with my silly monkey question after she'd referred to the delicate balancing act between economic growth and environmental sustainability to make the segue sound natural and spontaneous. But her improvised anecdote about visiting a new aquaponics farm in Singapore and how it had reminded her of an Australian farmstay with her kids had blindsided me.

When her story ended with her stepping in cow shit, she got a sincere and authentic laugh from us. She was funny. And I had forgotten about my monkey intervention.

Only Slick Scholar's wide eyes and a concerned nod brought me back into the room. I quickly said, 'Well, I haven't stepped in cow dung, only monkey poop, which is much smaller, but that's a competition I'm happy to lose.'

'Yes, my kids loved your monkey video,' said Female Minister. 'How many views has it had now?'

'More than two million,' I said.

'Yes, it's gone international now, too,' said Mr Loud, eagerly. He wasn't involved with the video, but he was still negotiating a new contract.

The Female Minister nodded her approval and said, 'Well, it certainly made me laugh. It's good to show a different side of Singapore.'

At the back of the studio, Slick Scholar couldn't stop grinning, mostly at me.

After the interview, Female Minister asked to take a selfie with the Rojak Breakfast Show crew, which had been discussed and approved in advance.

Then she asked to take a selfie just with me, to show her kids, which had not been discussed and approved in advance.

The executive of something or other from the Female Minister's office flapped around the studio at this unexpected turn of events.

This selfie wasn't on the pre-approved itinerary.

The Female Minister put her arm around me. Her security stiffened slightly. Maybe she was worried I might go for my concealed banana.

But we smiled for her camera, and I silently thanked my mother. I had not worn anything fattening.

Day 115

Slick Scholar sent an email to The Rojak Breakfast Show crew this morning, praising us for our 'professionalism', our 'outstanding journalism' and for 'making the most of our media scoop'.

Our media scoop came from the Female Minister's office.

Our outstanding journalism came from asking pre-approved questions from a cheat sheet.

Our professionalism came from listening to pre-approved answers from a cheat sheet.

They might as well give me the Pulitzer Prize now.

In the afternoon, Slick Scholar sent out a second email, congratulating Lauren Lam on being promoted to deputy editor of the lifestyle department.

We had drinks after work to celebrate.

I toasted Lauren's promotion. She toasted my new BFF in government.

On days like this, I think about the sheepish teenager scribbling down headlines in the back of her exercise book, dreaming of her first byline. She'd be so happy.

Day 120

My last day at the Rojak Breakfast Show. When I started, my media snobbery saw Loud and Louder as sad middle-aged men making fools of themselves. Now I see them as kind and decent middle-aged men making fools of themselves.

They had a cake delivered to the studio with 'Good Luck, Monkey Girl' written on the top in vanilla icing.

Mr Loud was in a particularly good mood. He had finally renewed his contract to continue the breakfast show. He was never going to be as popular as Mr Louder, but he still had a mortgage to pay off.

Mr Louder licked the vanilla icing off his fingers and assured me the best was yet to come. He said, 'I'm taking you out tonight, my treat.'

He didn't elaborate further.

Mr Loud pulled me aside and said, 'Don't get drunk with him.'

He didn't elaborate further.

After the show, Smooth Voice had to give a performance appraisal for my two-month stint in radio media.

He said, 'Yeah, good job, Millie. You didn't screw up.'

Then he left for a smoke break.

Around 10pm, I experienced Mr Louder's *treat*. He took me to Heaven.

I quickly discovered that Heaven is one of Singapore's most popular gay bars. I learned that Mr Louder is one of Singapore's most popular gay men.

And I found out that The Rojak Breakfast Show is popular among Singapore's gay men.

So I wasn't entirely surprised by the VIP treatment when I arrived. But I was taken aback when the doorman referred to me as 'Monkey Girl'.

It became a theme of the night. The doorman, the bartenders, the dancers and even the drag acts called me 'Monkey Girl'. But I loved the attention, especially after six cocktails. The music was good, the atmosphere was friendly and the sweaty crowd was half-naked.

One ridiculously chiselled guy, stripped to the waist, wandered over to me and Mr Louder at the bar, waving his wallet.

He said, 'Let me buy you a drink.'

His directness threw me off guard. 'No thanks,' I said.

He looked embarrassed and said, 'Sorry, ah, I was actually asking Mr Louder.'

Mr Louder revelled in my public embarrassment.

'No one cares about your tits here, Monkey Girl,' he shouted over the music.

He wasn't wrong. The men were more interested in each other's chests than mine. Mr Louder threw his arms in the air and started dancing at the bar. I was aware that everyone around us was watching.

I said, 'Aren't you worried they'll take photos?'

Mr Louder downed his vodka and said, 'Let them take photos, Monkey Girl. Both sides.'

He twirled around.

I reminded him that he was a Singaporean artiste.

He laughed and said, 'Not in here, Monkey Girl. In here, I'm just another guy having a good time. And I'm legal now. We're all fucking legal.'

'That's right,' said Ridiculously Chiselled Guy, before leading Mr Louder onto the dancefloor.

They looked so happy together. Everyone did. Suddenly, I felt like an imposter. This was their time and place, not mine.

Mr Louder had removed his shirt and was swinging it above his head like a lasso, so he wasn't going anywhere. I decided to discreetly slip away.

I made my way through the packed bar, trying not to get a shaved nipple in the eye when I felt a tap on the shoulder.

A friendly voice said, 'Well, at least let me buy you a drink first.'

Slick Scholar looked even more out of place than usual.

First, he wasn't sweaty.

And second, he still had his shirt on.

My national editor quickly registered my surprise. He said, 'No, I'm not gay. Mr Louder told me that you were coming here so I thought I'd come in to congratulate you.'

He took out his phone and showed me a WhatsApp message.

'Tell Miss Lee that I really enjoyed our chat.'

It wasn't from the Female Minister's office. It was from the

Female Minister herself.

Slick Scholar said, 'What a way to end your radio stint, eh?'

I felt myself blushing at both the compliment and Slick Scholar's influence. He was on texting terms with government ministers.

I said, 'Wow, that's nice.'

Slick Scholar suddenly found me hilarious. He said, 'That's all you can say? That's nice?'

'Well, it is.'

The compliment was nice, like his shoes were nice and his hair was nice. But his smile was something else.

'Yeah, I suppose it is,' said Slick Scholar, checking his reflection in the mirror behind the bar. 'Worth a drink at least.'

I checked on Mr Louder. He had disappeared, presumably taking Ridiculously Chiselled Guy with him. There was no need to make the night awkward for anyone.

I said, 'Yeah, but not here. Let's go somewhere quieter.'

On the way out, I spotted a familiar face sitting in a darkened booth. We waved at each other and then Uncle Groper went back to his friends.

THE PROBATION

Part III: Television Media

December – January

Day 120

I prepared for my first day in TV media by sleeping with my big boss.

After drinks in a Chinatown bar, Slick Scholar had offered to drop me home in a taxi, but I'd asked to see his East Coast apartment instead.

It was surprisingly sparse, like a photo shoot for an interior design magazine. He obviously wasn't home much. There wasn't much to see, so we found something else to do instead.

It was a fun night, or an improved night, at least.

Slick Scholar looked, sounded and smelled better than Hokkien Half-Ball. And he didn't sing football songs after sex.

He wanted to talk to me instead. About *me*.

At first, I thought he was doing that sensitive new man pillow talk that only happens in movies, where a Ryan Gosling-type leans on his elbow and moves the fringe away from the face of an Emma Stone-type as they contemplate a shared future.

When I slept with Hokkien Half-Ball, he sneezed on the sheets, complained about his morning allergies and then emptied his nostrils in the hotel sink.

But Slick Scholar really was different.

After sex, he sat up in bed and watched me return from the bathroom. He said, 'you've got nice legs.'

'Oh shut up,' I said, pretending I didn't care. I did.

He said, 'You really do. I noticed that when you joined.'

I flopped onto the bed beside him and asked why he hadn't done anything about it. He said, 'I'm your boss and I'm not Hokkien Half-Ball. I believe a work-life separation is important.'

I rolled my eyes and said, 'That sounded a bit rehearsed. We're lying in your bed. So you don't believe in a work-life separation that much, right?'

'I do,' he said, sitting up straight.

He still had the physique of an elite school athlete. I asked what had changed his mind.

He thought about my question by scratching the top of his left shoulder, which showed off his right bicep. He caught me staring. He knew what he was doing. He said, 'You did. You changed my perception of you.'

'How?'

He said, 'When what happened with you and Hokkien Half-Ball *happened*. I thought, *aiyoh*, another one.'

I turned bright red at the mention of Hokkien Half-Ball, which made me loathe the asshole even more. Slick Scholar ignored my glowing face, which made me like him just a little more.

Still, I wasn't entirely sure what he meant. I said, 'Another what? Another slut?'

Slick Scholar sighed, as if he felt sorry for me. He said, 'No *lah*, another one for *him*. I know what he's like. And Peranakan Pervert. It's the culture.'

'Then stop it,' I said firmly.

He looked surprised and said, 'Stop what? No one has complained. No one went to senior management. We can't react to rumours. We had nothing to react against. Until you.'

I pointed out that it wasn't an easy decision.

He nodded and said, 'I know. And when you filed a complaint. That's when I knew.'

'What?'

He edged closer and said, 'That you were more than a pair of legs.'

I hit him with a pillow. 'Sexist bastard.'

'What? I like tough heartlanders like you,' he said, shielding himself from my pillow attack. 'Tough heartlanders work harder.'

'Ah, now you're a patronising bastard, is it?' I hit him again with the pillow.

Then he whacked me with his pillow.

Then we wrestled around on the bed for a bit.

Then he leaned over me and said, 'You really are sexy though. It's those eyes.'

The line was lame, but he kissed me anyway.

And then he said, 'You must expect resentment from the other TV journalists. You're prettier than them. They won't look like you on camera.'

I asked Slick Scholar what I was going to look like on camera. He pinned my wrists gently to the bed and said, 'Like sex.'

The line was just as lame as the last one, but the feeling was mutual.

So we had sex again and then I hurried home, promising to keep things discreet and professional at work.

And Slick Scholar promised to give me TV assignments that my talent deserved.

In the afternoon, I met Ang Moh Accent outside the State Courts.

Ang Moh Accent was a local TV legend. He was around fifty but had retained his boyish good looks. He reminded me of Jay Chou.

He was famous for his smooth delivery, which belonged in a Shakespeare play. He was Singaporean but had gone to Anglo-Chinese School. Obviously.

Despite the intense humidity, he wore a dark suit and a crisp white shirt on the steps of the State Courts, which was a little over the top – he dressed more formally than our politicians – but it was his signature look.

When he shook my hand and introduced himself, he practically spat at me. He over-enunciated every vowel and consonant.

His voice sounded very posh. His overly expressive face suggested he needed a shit.

He said, 'You must be Millie. I've heard a lot about you.'

I wondered why.

'The bosses love you,' he said. 'You must be *good*.'

He emphasised the last word, which only played into my paranoia. I wasn't sure if he was somehow aware that I'd recently had sex with our boss, or he was over-enunciating again to sound like Benedict Cumberbatch.

'I've done OK so far,' I said.

Ang Moh Accent looked me up and down. 'I'm sure,' he said.

When he'd finished patronising my appearance, he started on my intellect.

He said, 'As you know, this has been a massive court case for the last two months.'

I lied and nodded sagely. In truth, I had spent most of the last two months either dressed as a durian or making up raps about farting. But I'd heard the headlines in the radio news.

Ang Moh Accent said, 'Scams are huge and this one has really captured the public's imagination. The woman fell in love with an African oil magnate, who was in Singapore to pick up his father's remains. But his dad hadn't really died and he was only barely in the oil business.'

'What did he do then?'

'He pumped petrol.'

According to Ang Moh Accent, the victim had transferred her CPF savings to her lover so he could fly his father's remains back to Africa. In return, her lover was going to give her a percentage of the family oil business.

The victim had lost almost half a million dollars.

The victim's case was being settled today.

The victim had to be interviewed outside the State Courts. No matter what.

And it was all up to me. A successful interview depended on my performance.

I had to hold up a lighting reflector.

Day 121

Until yesterday, I didn't know what a lighting reflector was.

Until yesterday, I could hold my arms above my head.

Today, I woke up with the sorest shoulders. I also woke up beside Slick Scholar.

He made me breakfast in bed – tea and kaya toast – and we watched Ang Moh Accent's interview with the scamming victim on a laptop.

Ang Moh Accent was impressive. His questioning technique was concise. His body language was empathetic. Looking like Jay Chou's big brother helped, but he had a knack for getting strangers to talk on camera.

'He is good,' I admitted, chomping my toast and spilling crumbs on the duvet.

'He is, but only because the lighting is good,' Slick Scholar said, giggling into his teacup.

I reminded him that I got a media scholarship.

Slick Scholar pointed his slice of toast at the screen and said, 'I can tell. Can win an Oscar for best cinematography already.'

I put down my toast and said, 'I'm just gonna hold that reflector for two months, right?'

'Of course not,' said Slick Scholar. 'You'll learn all aspects of TV reporting.'

Day 122

I didn't hold up a lighting reflector today. I held up a boom mic instead.

For three hours. In Orchard Road.

Ang Moh Accent did a piece on Orchard Road's Christmas lights.

Ang Moh Accent is a natural on camera, but even he struggled to conjure any words beyond 'colourful', 'dazzle' and 'festive'.

Day 123

There was an online news story written to go alongside Ang Moh Accent's video clip. The headline read, 'Orchard Road dazzles for festive fun.'

There was presumably no room left for 'colourful'.

Day 124

In the morning, the TV team received a letter of complaint. A viewer claimed that our 'crass emphasis on a vulgar lights display underlined the commercialisation of a sacred, religious occasion.'

In the afternoon, Slick Scholar sent a congratulatory note. The official sponsors of the Orchard Road Christmas lights had enjoyed Ang Moh Accent's coverage.

In fact, they were effusive in their praise.

They were also regular advertisers during our commercial breaks.

Day 126

Slick Scholar sent me out on my first independent assignment today. I suspect he had three reasons for doing so.

First, Ang Moh Accent had been given the day off to host a pro-Government event at a local community club.

Second, the risks were minimal. My assignment was an ongoing event and a piece to camera – or PTC, as I now call it, being a professional TV reporter and everything. There were no interviews required.

If I messed up, the editors could just slap a voiceover across the footage.

And third, the sex had been particularly good last night.

I'd like to think this was a bonus, rather than part of the job description.

The event was being held outside VivoCity, a shopping centre mostly used by the rich living around HarbourFront and teenagers and blur tourists.

On the way over, I shared a taxi with Chain-Smoking Chinese Cameraman.

Chain-Smoking Chinese Cameraman looked like a skeleton with tattoos. He didn't stop shaking, presumably because he was suffering from nicotine withdrawal. He'd smoked continuously whilst waiting for the taxi.

On the back seat, he fiddled with his lenses and said, 'This one easy *lah*. Just talk a bit during toilet break. Nothing to say. Same shit every year.'

I agreed with him.

We were going to cover the 'Stand and Deliver the COE' endurance challenge, which is as ridiculous as it sounds.

I've never understood Singapore's obsessions with these things. When I was a kid, I remember seeing a group of people leaning on cars outside Ngee Ann City for hours and hours, trying to outlast each other. The last person standing won the car, but not always the Certificate of Entitlement (the COE).

The COE is often worth more than the value of the car, so a marketing genius came up with the brilliant idea of getting participants to stand on the certificate of entitlement, i.e. an actual piece of A4 paper.

The 'Stand and Deliver the COE' endurance challenge involves a hundred people standing on pieces of A4 outside VivoCity.

The COE is mostly an online document now, rather than a physical piece of paper, but never let facts get in the way of a crazy marketing story.

The COE doesn't come with a car either, only a certificate, so the eventual winner would still need to buy a vehicle afterwards.

The COE, as a piece of paper, is tiny, so referees, or moderators, or sad individuals, whatever you want to call them, are employed to walk around and determine if the competitors' feet are entirely inside the piece of A4. The competitors may only step off the paper once every six hours for a toilet break.

The competition penalises anyone with a weak bladder.

The competition penalises anyone with big feet.

The competition rewards anyone who might be insane.

By the time Chain-Smoking Chinese Cameraman had set me up with a mic, ready to record, the competitors had been rooted to the same spot for almost a full day.

I closed my eyes and took a deep breath. I was about to address the nation for the first time. When Lee Kuan Yew addressed the nation, he famously cried on camera. I knew how he felt.

When Chain-Smoking Chinese Cameraman gave me the nod, I spoke my first words as a TV reporter. I said, 'It's coming down to the wire here at the "Stand and Deliver the COE" endurance challenge. After twenty-one hours, we are left with just seven competitors. We lost the eighth competitor moments ago, when he accidentally peed himself and was disqualified. But they're all about to get wet soon as heavy rain is forecast. A stormy night is going to make it very hard for the remaining competitors to rise and shine in the morning. Back to you in the studio.'

Chain-Smoking Chinese Cameraman shook his head and whispered, 'So random.'

Slick Scholar reviewed the footage back in the office and then called and asked me to shoot the clip again without referring to a participant pissing himself, as the organiser was a regular advertiser during our commercial breaks.

Besides, Mother Superior had already reviewed the piece and thought my PTC contained too much sexual innuendo. But then, she found sexual innuendo in everything, presumably because she didn't find sexual intercourse anywhere.

My second take was decent, until the excitable emcee started screaming at the crowd.

My third take came out shaky because Chain-Smoking Chinese Cameraman was missing his smoke break.

My fourth take was perfect, until a contestant collapsed over my shoulder.

Luckily, Chain-Smoking Chinese Cameraman had captured the whole thing. He'd followed the stricken man from his initial collapse until the ambulance arrived. The footage had 'viral' stamped across it.

But Slick Scholar rejected the clip.

The organiser was a regular advertiser during our commercial breaks. In the end, the editors ran some bland footage with a generic voiceover.

My voice was not included.

Day 127

My face and voice went out on the national news for the first time today.

Standing in the rain, I filled TV screens across the country and said, 'The Stand and Deliver the COE endurance challenge reached its fortieth hour today and we are down to the last two contestants. I'm here with one of them now. Can you tell me how you feel?'

Weary Chinese Man said, 'Tired. So tired.'

I asked how he felt after reaching the final two. Weary Chinese Man said, 'Very good.'

I asked what he'd do if he won the COE. Weary Chinese Man said, 'Buy a car *lor*.'

Chain-Smoking Chinese Cameraman and I then dashed across the forecourt outside VivoCity to interview the other remaining contestant, who was standing about ten metres away on his sodden piece of A4 paper.

I asked how he planned to outlast his final opponent. Weary Malay Man said, 'Cannot fall asleep.'

I asked what his strategy was for staying awake after forty long hours. Weary Malay Man said, 'Mus' keep eyes open.'

I turned back to the camera. I was dripping wet. I peered through the pouring rain and said, 'As you can see, both men are determined to get their hands on that coveted COE. And neither man looks ready to quit. Back to you in the studio.'

When Chain-Smoking Chinese Cameraman was packing away his equipment, he said, 'What's coveted ah?'

When Mother Superior cleared the clip, she reminded me to use simple English.

When Slick Scholar and I watched the clip in bed later, he said I'd make a decent wet T-shirt contestant.

Day 128

The 'Stand and Deliver the COE' Endurance Challenge ended today. After 55 hours and 17 minutes, Weary Malay Man was crowned the winner and collected a piece of paper worth more than $100,000.

He now owns a certificate that entitles him to a large car.

He just needs to find another $60k or so to buy a large car.

After 55 hours and 19 minutes, I was expected to conduct a coherent interview with a man who hadn't slept for three days.

I said, 'Congratulations on becoming the inaugural Stand and

Deliver the COE Endurance Challenge. How do you feel?'

My question was long, but I had been instructed to give the full and proper title at every mention. The organiser was a regular advertiser during our commercial breaks.

Weary Malay Man said, 'My mind is so happy, but my body feel like shit.'

The second part of his sentence was chopped off in the edit, reducing his verbal contribution to five words, which was probably for the best. The contestants' brains were fried.

After 55 hours and 16 minutes, Weary Chinese Man was disqualified when he started hallucinating, jumping off his A4 piece of paper to avoid getting bitten by the snake.

There was no snake, obviously, but I recorded a quick piece, just in case, even though I knew there was no chance of it going to air.

The organiser was a regular advertiser during our commercial breaks.

As I recorded Weary Chinese Man's dramatic disqualification, he could be seen over my shoulder, running away and ordering event organisers to 'whack the python'.

Day 129

The 'Stand and Deliver the COE' endurance challenge went viral today, but it had nothing to do with me.

A spectator had recorded the snake scene on his phone and sent it to an independent news site.

There were rumours that he'd also sent the clip to our newsroom, but we had opted not to run it, as the organiser was a regular advertiser during our commercial breaks.

By lunchtime, 'whack the python' was trending across all social media platforms.

By evening, 'whack the python' was trending in Malaysia and Indonesia.

By midnight, 'whack the python' was trending on the *Daily Mail* website in the UK.

Day 131

The National Parks Board issued a press release today, assuring concerned residents that a python was not on the loose around HarbourFront.

Members of the public were also reminded not to whack our native wildlife.

Ang Moh Accent and I had been instructed not to do a follow-up piece for camera, as the organiser was a regular advertiser during our commercial breaks.

The consensus was the surreal turn of events would soon be forgotten.

Day 133

Overnight, American talk show host Stephen Colbert showed the viral clip of Weary Chinese Man on *The Late Show*.

Colbert's studio audience repeatedly chanted, 'Whack the python! Whack the python!'

At 9am sharp, Captain Mayhem called an emergency meeting with the major editors and me and Chain-Smoking Chinese Cameraman.

Independent news sites were having a field day, mocking our sanitised coverage of the runner-up's disqualification.

Our CEO decided to pick on the easiest target first, which was a mistake, as Chain-Smoking Chinese Cameraman didn't appreciate being denied nicotine for a pointless meeting.

Captain Mayhem said, 'Did you not film the contestant's meltdown?'

'Got,' said Chain-Smoking Chinese Cameraman.

Captain Mayhem said, 'And it was usable footage?'

'Yeah *lah*,' said China-Smoking Chinese Cameraman gruffly. His professionalism was being questioned. Plus, he really wanted a cigarette.

Captain Mayhem said, 'Then we should have used the footage. We are being scooped at events where we are the official media partner. How can this happen?'

All eyes in the room were on me. I said, 'We filmed the whole thing. The guy leaping off the paper, hallucinating, screaming at the organisers. Everything. I did a piece on it. But ...'

I didn't want to incriminate anyone else in the room, especially the man I was sleeping with.

Finally, Slick Scholar said, 'I made the decision not to run it.'

Captain Mayhem was clearly irritated and demanded to know why.

'The arrangement is delicate,' said Slick Scholar. 'The TV advertising was part of an overall package.'

Captain Mayhem wanted to know more about this overall package.

Slick Scholar whispered into Captain Mayhem's ear. Captain Mayhem started leaking from his forehead. 'Right, yes, understand,' he stuttered. 'It's delicate.'

Like an idiot, I raised my hand and asked, 'What's delicate?'

Captain Mayhem said, 'Advertising, Millie. We put a package together across our platforms for the client. TV coverage was part of that package.'

I said, 'Isn't that, like, client journalism?'

Mother Superior raised an eyebrow. 'Someone went to university,' she whispered.

'Client journalism typically relates to politicians, not advertisers,' Slick Scholar said.

He then said, 'To pay good journalists, we need good advertising.'

'Exactly,' said Captain Mayhem. 'We need revenue. But I also want our journalists to cover these big stories. So if a story like this breaks again, I want us to break it first.'

'Well, maybe check with us first,' said Slick Scholar.

'Yes, just check with us first,' agreed Captain Mayhem.

Day 134

After Captain Mayhem's inspirational pep talk, I was allowed to do an investigative follow-up piece.

I interviewed Weary Chinese Man in his hospital bed. The organisers of the 'Stand and Deliver the COE' endurance challenge had organised the interview.

In fact, three of their bosses stood around the bed as they presented the bewildered patient with a cheque for $55,016 – a reward for his standing effort of 55 hours and 16 minutes, which made no sense mathematically.

I asked him how he felt about the unexpected prize.

He said, 'I'd like to thank the organisers of the "Stand and Deliver the COE" endurance challenge for their generosity.'

He almost sounded human.

Not that it mattered. The hospital interview didn't trend on social media.

After the news went out in the evening, Captain Mayhem popped down to the studio. He said, 'You showed good restraint in your interview, Millie. It's not the right time to say things like "whack the python" on local TV.'

I'd love to know when it was.

Day 136

Before half the office went off for their Christmas holidays, Slick

Scholar called an informal, inspirational lunch meeting with all the remaining editors and journalists. According to Lauren, quite a few had resigned since the last informal, inspirational lunch meeting.

She sat beside me, gorging on her nasi padang and offering her personal take on proceedings.

Apparently, Slick Scholar usually organised these relaxed get-togethers when there was something seriously stressful and formal to be discussed.

She was right. Our national editor wanted to focus on the latest findings from a media survey, organised by a prestigious consultancy firm.

According to the survey results, a majority of Singaporeans still trusted local news brands over international news brands.

But the numbers were declining. In fact, all the numbers were declining. Our readership, listenership and viewership figures were all down. Even the public trust percentages were heading in the wrong direction.

Slick Scholar reminded us, quite forcefully I felt, that if we were unable to speak truth to power, our media platforms would lose credibility among the public.

Our media had to remain truthful. Our media had to remain trusted. Our media had to remain relevant.

He would stand up for us. He would protect us. If truth was on our side, we had nothing to fear.

I can't lie. His speech was genuinely inspirational. I went home feeling rather good about my chosen profession and was eager to tell my parents.

But my Mum was watching a Korean drama on Netflix.

And my Dad was watching a TikTok rap called 'Whack the Python'.

Day 137

Our media rivals have gone to town with the latest media survey findings. Independent news sites boasted about their rising readership. They ignored the fact that their public trust percentages were lower than ours, so Slick Scholar instructed the editors to play up that angle in our coverage.

I was sent to Raffles Place to get vox pops on the topic of media trust in Singapore. Vox pops allow members of the public to share their honest opinions with a wide audience.

The problem is Singaporeans don't like to share their honest opinions with a wide audience.

They save them for small audiences at reunion dinners.

Chain-Smoking Chinese Cameraman was on medical leave. He had a chest infection.

So I went with Chain-Smoking Malay Cameraman instead. He was just as skinny as Chain-Smoking Chinese Cameraman but had fewer tattoos.

Together, we stood in the midday sun at a half-empty Raffles Place, a week before Christmas, trying to get soundbites from white collar workers who didn't want to speak as they rushed to lunch appointments.

Raffles Place was often a go-to destination for vox pops, as the area had an international, predominantly English-speaking crowd. Expats were generally more willing to speak, but I needed locals. Finally, I caught one, sitting beside the grass, finishing his coffee.

I said, 'Hi, I'm reporter Millie Lee. Can I ask you a quick question about the Singapore media.'

He said, 'Sure.'

I said, 'What do you think about the Singapore media?'

He said, 'Never read it.'

I needed to change tack. I approached a young Chinese woman, around my age, hoping for a little sistership or something. She saw the globs of sweat running down my cheeks and clearly felt sorry for me. She agreed to a short interview.

I said, 'How often do you read or watch the news?'

She said, 'Every day. On the MRT to work. And again, on the way home.'

I said, 'That's great. Which news sites do you read?'

She said, 'Mostly CNN.'

After four hours, I found six interviewees willing to discuss their local news consumption. Three of them used our media platforms. The other three preferred our rivals.

A Singaporean uncle told me that 'the Singapore media had been controlled by the PAP since LKY's time' and I needed to get another job.

A Singaporean auntie told me to wear less makeup in the hot sun and gave me a packet of tissues.

A kid asked if he could say hello to his friends on camera and an Australian banker asked if I was free after work.

Back in the office, the editors picked the three supporters of our news content, making sure we were namechecked in their vox pops.

The editors also picked one of the interviewees who preferred watching our rival news organisation, which was not namechecked.

Slick Scholar said, 'We gotta be balanced, but I'm not giving the bastards free publicity.'

After work, I went for a drink with Lauren. I needed one after a long, sweaty day. When I arrived, Lauren had already downed a few and had moved onto shots. She ordered a couple more from the barman, who she couldn't stop flirting with, and dragged me over to a quiet booth.

I said, 'Wah, you seem happy?'

She said, 'Today, I got my first pay cheque as a deputy lifestyle editor. I can retire already. *Not.*'

She raised her shot glass in the air. She looked a little pissed.

I said, 'That's great though. You settled into the new job so fast.'

She said, 'Yeah. It's faster when you shag the editor.'

Lauren downed her shot and slammed the glass on the table. She waved at the barman and called for another. He responded immediately, which was hardly surprising. Lauren's cleavage was practically smiling at him.

She peered into my eyes, waiting for some sort of response. She said, 'Got nothing to say, ah?'

I said, 'I'm just a bit shocked. Hokkien Half-Ball, ah?'

She nodded and slapped the table as the barman arrived with

another two shots. I still hadn't touched my first. Lauren downed hers as I tried to unscramble my thoughts.

I asked her why.

'He asked me,' she shrugged. 'He's always asking.'

I didn't need Lauren's raised eyebrow. I realised how pathetically hypocritical I sounded as soon as the words had left my mouth.

She said, 'You're gonna preach to me, is it?'

'No, of course not,' I said. 'But at least I didn't know he was married.'

I sounded like a whiny brat, trying to defend myself.

Lauren said, 'It's just a bit of fun, OK? His wife doesn't care, as long as he doesn't embarrass her.'

'Wow.'

'Are you judging me?'

'No *lah*, but what if he embarrasses you? He bloody embarrassed me. He never told me about his wife.'

'That's why,' said Lauren. 'I know about his wife and kids.'

She caught the barman's eye again and called for another round. She said, 'It's just a bit of fun.'

'Is it? You seem drunk already. On your own.'

She seemed to stop acting. She stopped grinning like an idiot. She said, 'Tonight was supposed to be our night. But she made him get the kids from tuition.'

'*Made* him? He's their father.' I leaned towards her. 'You know he bet on me, right? With Peranakan Pervert. They had a bet to see who could screw me first.'

She said, 'Peranakan Pervert has gone already.'

I didn't know how to respond to that. It wasn't really my

place to say anything. Lauren was older than me. She had been a journalist longer than me. She knew how the industry worked and she was making it work for her.

Eventually, I mumbled, 'Yeah, fair enough. I cannot be a hypocrite, right?'

She was probably thinking about the awkward fact that I had once slept with Hokkien Half-Ball, her current boss, who also happened to be her current lover.

But I was actually thinking about the awkward fact that I was currently sleeping with *my* boss.

Lauren said, 'We're just having a good time.' She sounded even less convincing now.

'Just be careful,' I said. 'Whatever they do outside, they always go back to their family.'

She brushed me away and said, 'Yeah *lah*, yeah *lah*, can we talk about something else now? I came here to get drunk with you, not get lectured. You heard about that superhero thing? We're the official media partner for the movie premiere. I'm doing a one-on-one interview with the actor. You should do a TV piece.'

Day 138

Slick Scholar sent me to Marina Bay Sands to interview the third lead in Lauren's superhero thing.

The lead actor was promoting the movie in Australia.

The second lead was doing the premiere in Tokyo.

So, Singapore got the third lead, a former child star on

American TV.

There's always a hierarchy for these things.

I was told to meet him by the Christmas tree display on the Marina Bay platform and use the dusky skyline as a backdrop. The Christmas trees were dressed in the colours of the movie's key characters. Marina Bay looked like it was being invaded by an army of hairy toy soldiers.

Chain-Smoking Chinese Camera Man was setting up his tripod when two American PR women with bright lanyards appeared and told us to sign a non-disclosure agreement. Then we were given bright wristbands and allowed into the roped-off media enclosure.

They also reminded us that we had five minutes.

We were not to go beyond the five minutes.

We were not to deviate from the pre-approved questions.

We were not to ask Third Lead about his love life.

Third Lead was nineteen years old.

The American women also told us where to stand and wait on the Marina Bay platform. Chain-Smoking Chinese Camera Man said, 'Are we in Singapore or not?'

PR Woman No. 1 said, 'I'm sorry?'

Chain-Smoking Chinese Camera Man turned away and muttered, 'Make me feel like a foreigner in my own country. Basket.'

PR Woman No.1 thought about a follow-up, but she was interrupted by a commotion near the stairs. Third Lead was on his way down. He stopped to wave at his teenage fans.

I counted six of them.

This was his first major movie.

Two security guards flanked the actor, making their way through a crowd that consisted of journalists, PR people, reps from the movie studio and an expat walking her dog.

PR Woman No.2 began to flap. She said, 'He's here. He's here.'

Chain-Smoking Chinese Man adjusted his lens and mumbled, '*Relak lah, ang moh.*' He was grouchy. He couldn't smoke on the Marina Bay event platform.

PR Woman No.1 ushered Third Lead towards the light of our TV camera, whispering in his ear the entire time. She said, 'We do TV first, then a sitdown interview for their website.'

Third Lead beamed at us with a pure white, all-American smile. 'Sure,' he said. Third Lead was charismatic. He made a point of shaking our hands, even grasping the nicotine-stained fingers of Chain-Smoking Chinese Cameraman, who was grudgingly won over.

'Yah, hallo,' said my cameraman, not bothering to look up from his lens.

PR Woman No.1 tapped her watch and said, 'OK, whenever you're ready.'

Chain-Smoking Chinese Cameraman pinned a mic to Third Lead's lapel and then dragged the actor by the elbow. 'Stand here ah,' he said to one of Hollywood's rising stars.

Chain-Smoking Chinese Cameraman checked his lens and gave me a nod. I took a breath and watched lifestyle and entertainment journalists from across Asia watching me, just over Third Lead's shoulder. I noticed Lauren had arrived. She was tapping her notepad but staring right at me. I smiled at her. She didn't smile back. I didn't have a notepad for reassurance. I had memorised my questions. I had even timed them. I had a polished five minutes prepped and ready to go.

I was a short interview away from a million international clicks on YouTube.

I said, 'Welcome to Singapore, Third Lead, is this your first time here?'

He said, 'Yeah, it's awesome. It's so hot and humid, but the fans are great.'

He waved up at them again. Six teenage girls waved back at him.

I said, 'What can you tell us about this movie?'

He said, 'Ah, it's got a lot of action. So much cool action, you know. Asians are in for a real treat.'

PR Woman No.1 muttered something off camera.

Third Lead nodded and said, '*Singaporeans* are in for a real treat.' PR Woman No.1 retreated.

I said, 'Have you had a chance to have Singaporean food yet?'

He said, 'Ah, yeah, I love Asian food.'

Third Lead caught the glare from PR Woman No.1. 'Especially *Singaporean* food,' he added.

I said, 'Really? What's been your favourite Singaporean dish so far?'

Off camera, PR Woman No.1 clucked at him. 'Chicken rice,' said Third Lead quickly. 'I love your chicken rice, man. I'm gonna get some straight after this. Maybe you can take me.'

PR Woman No.1 stopped clucking and turned her glare towards me. In the background, Lauren didn't look too impressed either.

Third Lead flashed his gleaming teeth at me. He said, 'Where can we get the best chicken rice in Singapore?'

I said, 'Maybe Lau Pa Sat, just across Marina Bay. Have you had a chance to speak Singlish yet?'

Third Lead paused to receive off-camera instructions from PR Woman No.1. He said, 'It's *lah*, right? I love the way you say "*lah*" at the end of sentences. Let's eat chicken rice *lah*.'

I could feel Chain-Smoking Chinese Cameraman suppress the urge to punch Third Lead.

I pressed on with the world's most excruciating interview. I said, 'What else do you hope to see in Singapore?'

Third Lead pointed up at the three hotel towers beside us and said, 'Marina Bay Sands. It looks amazing. It's an amazing hotel.'

Marina Bay Sands was the official hotel partner for the movie event.

PR Woman No.2 appeared in my eyeline and gave me the universal signal to wrap it up.

I said, 'And finally, what's been your favourite thing about Singapore?'

Third Lead gestured towards the crowd of journalists, the PR staff, movie studio executives and that expat woman waiting for her dog to finish peeing up a palm tree. He said, 'The people. From the moment I arrived, the Singaporean people have been totally amazing to me.'

He'd been in Singapore for three hours.

Chain-Smoking Chinese Cameraman stepped away from his camera and pulled the mic from Third Lead's lapel. 'Thanks ah,' he growled, before disappearing for a smoke break.

The American PR women tried to steer their Hollywood rice bowl towards Lauren, who was waiting on a bench. Third Lead appeared to be in no hurry though. He was hanging back. He said, 'That was fun, Millie. And I was serious about that chicken rice. I'll be done in an hour.'

I said, 'Thanks for the offer. But I've got to go back to the office and edit your interview.'

Third Lead shook off his minders and leered at me. 'Come on, it's Christmas. Come to the hotel when you're done. I've got a suite.'

'And I've got a boyfriend.'

Third Lead left without saying another word.

Day 139

Lauren was seriously pissed with me today.

Apparently, her interview with Third Lead did not go well. Their time together was cut short, and he barely answered her questions. Her feature was downgraded to a short Q&A. Hokkien Half-Ball had to write a colour piece about the superhero premiere to fill the space that had been originally allocated to Lauren. The new deputy lifestyle editor felt that a) she'd been professionally humiliated and b) it was all my fault.

According to Lauren, her interview subject only became surly after I'd rejected his dodgy dinner offer.

I said, 'So I have to go to his hotel suite so you get a good story, is it?'

I should not have raised my voice. We had gone to a posh café near our office. A family on the next table stopped eating to listen in to our conversation.

Lauren didn't seem to care. She said, 'He asked you for *makan*. Would've made for a great story.'

I asked who for.

Lauren seemed really agitated. She stirred her coffee and said, 'For you and me. I needed to write a good one.'

I insisted that her Q&A had been a fun read.

She banged her teaspoon against the wooden tabletop. 'It was shit,' she said. 'He gave me the lead feature and I messed it up. I got enough people in the office giving me shit.'

'What for?'

Lauren looked around the café. The place was more expensive than a hawker centre and popular with the editors who had enough time and money to eat there. There were usually journalists huddled together around tables, bitching about the company and promising to leave as soon as a better-paid job came along, one that allowed them to sit in a fancy café for hours, bitching about the company.

Lauren waited until she was satisfied that no one important was eavesdropping. She said, 'I got promoted too fast. There were others ahead of me.'

I said, 'Maybe that's because you're a better writer.'

Lauren looked at me like I was a dumb kid. 'Yeah right,' she said. 'He had to promote me.'

'Hokkien Half-Ball?'

She blushed this time and said, 'Yeah. I kept giving him shit about his wife. So he gave me a promotion.'

I wasn't sure what the appropriate response was, so I played safe. I said, 'That's good, right?'

'Only if I deserve it,' she said. 'My stories must lead the lifestyle section. They've got to trend. The others are already making comments. Even Mother Superior. She was destroying my piece as usual, kept asking why was I deputy lifestyle editor already, if I can only write simple Q&A.'

I pretended to find something interesting at the bottom of my coffee cup. 'You could've said no,' I muttered.

'To what?'

'To the promotion. To Hokkien Half-Ball.'

'Oh, like you did?'

'I made a mistake.'

'Yeah, and you went straight to the bosses and fixed it, 'cos they all love you. Some of us don't have a choice like you.'

Lauren made me blush, but not because I was embarrassed. I knew that she was right.

I did have a choice. I chose to report Hokkien Half-Ball and Peranakan Pervert.

I chose to just meet Lauren for a quick coffee because I knew that I was meeting Slick Scholar for dinner.

I chose to be a hypocrite.

I assured Lauren that everything would work out fine. She didn't believe me, which was totally understandable. I didn't really believe myself.

At dinner, Slick Scholar spent an hour talking about his thwarted career plans, how his youth and preternatural ability worked against him, how his path was being blocked by cronies like Captain Mayhem and other old farts trying to protect their rice bowls.

He wasn't really chatting with me. He was talking *at* me. The dinner was more of a Ted Talk than a date. He did eventually seek my opinion about the food. I felt like one of those giddy Ted Talk audience members who gets a question picked.

He also complimented my tight top, presumably because he intended to have sex later. But I gently pointed out that it was the wrong time of the month, so he quickly returned to his life goals and long-term political aspirations.

I was lying about the wrong time of the month. But my lunch and dinner discussions were about as much fun as a period headache.

When I got home, I found my mother sitting alone at her beloved mahjong table. She had planned to play with my father and their friends.

But he had been called away on urgent business. In Batam.

Day 140

On my way to work this morning, I listened to The Rojak Breakfast Show. I had developed a real soft spot for the guys. Loud and Louder had ruled the airwaves since I was in primary school, but I'd never tuned in until my radio stint with them. Plus, Mr Louder had sent me a WhatsApp message, tipping me off that Third Lead was going to make an unannounced guest appearance before heading off to Changi Airport. (The early reviews for the superhero movie have been terrible. Last-minute publicity was hastily arranged in a bid to give the opening weekend a boost.) Listening on the MRT, I giggled when Mr Louder made a sly dig on my behalf. He said, 'So, Third Lead, what do you think of the young ladies in Singapore?'

'They are very nice,' said Third Lead, unconvincingly.

Mr Louder kept going. He said, 'Did you meet anyone nice at Marina Bay?'

Third Lead laughed. His fake laughing was as bad as his acting. He said, 'They were all nice at Marina Bay, but I kept things professional.'

'That's not what I heard,' said Mr Louder.

He'd heard differently from me. He had nicknamed me one of his 'gossip bitches' and we had texted back and forth after the Marina Bay cringe fest.

To his credit, Third Lead played along. He said, 'They all rejected me. Looks like I'll be all alone at Christmas.'

The DJs pretended to sympathise, commiserating with the poor Hollywood martyr. The banter was cheesy, but inoffensive for an easily offended audience. I missed doing the show with the guys.

And then Mr Louder said, 'Come on ah, Third Lead. No need to be so modest. You are very handsome. If you asked me, I wouldn't say no.'

I didn't miss the show with the guys now.

As Mr Loud laughed awkwardly and quickly thanked Third Lead for coming in, I knew what was coming next.

Day 141

Mr Louder has been temporarily dropped from The Rojak Breakfast Show for 'inappropriate content'.

Our radio station has apologised for the 'inappropriate content'.

Religious organisations and pro-family groups have come forward to condemn the 'inappropriate content'.

Our competitors have found experts to say that our radio station may be fined for the 'inappropriate content'.

My father said I should be ashamed to work for people who put out such 'inappropriate content' – and then made another important business call to Batam.

Day 143

Captain Mayhem called an emergency meeting with the editors this morning. A decision was taken to release a detailed press release with another apology for the 'inappropriate content', but that would be the end of the matter. He wanted no further comment from anyone within our organisation.

At lunchtime, Captain Mayhem approved the following press release.

'In view of the public feedback, we have tasked our

regulatory committee to investigate the circumstances surrounding the "inappropriate content" that went out on the Rojak Breakfast Show during an unscheduled, improvised interview.

While the tone of the show has always been playful and occasionally humorous, we acknowledge our responsibility in providing content that protects younger audiences. We must remain sensitive to societal norms and values and avoid age-inappropriate content.

Counselling will be made available to Mr Louder, if required, and all our DJs will be briefed again on the Content Code for Radio Services.

We'd like to thank our audience, once again, for their considered feedback and wish them all a very happy holiday.'

At 1pm, Slick Scholar amended the press release to remove Mr Louder's name.

At 2pm, Hokkien Half-Ball suggested it was a bit crass to wish everyone a happy holiday.

At 3pm, Mother Superior was uncomfortable with the close juxtaposition between the 'inappropriate content' and 'younger audiences'. She said the paragraphs hinted at paedophilia. (She really can find the disturbing in anything.)

At 4pm, the press release was cleared for publication, subject to any final amendments from Captain Mayhem's close friends.

At 5pm, our rival news organisations wondered why we were taking so long to issue a press release, speculating that there was something to hide.

At 6pm, Captain Mayhem demanded to know why our news organisation was taking so long to follow up on a story where the only source involved was our news organisation.

At 7pm, Slick Scholar had a private chat with Captain Mayhem, delicately pointing out that the apologetic press release didn't include an apology. Captain Mayhem refused to make further amendments, angrily pointing out that he was already a meme on TikTok.

At 7.15pm, the press release was published on our website.

At 9.25pm, Mr Louder was rushed to hospital.

Day 144

According to the press release, Mr Louder had collapsed from nervous exhaustion. He was recovering in hospital.

Our employer pledged its full support. The same employer that had suspended him for 'inappropriate content'.

The relevant media authority published a few kind words. The same authority that had reaffirmed its position on what constituted 'inappropriate content'.

At a hastily convened meeting, Slick Scholar reminded all journalists not to speculate on our colleague's well-being. Apparently, the editors had sent flowers and chocolates, via a delivery service. The editors wanted to respect Mr Louder's privacy at such a difficult time.

They also knew that rival media companies had staked out the hospital and didn't want to be photographed going in.

There were rumours flying around the office that hardly anyone had visited Mr Louder.

His family did not approve of his 'inappropriate content' either.

I was in no mood to face a camera. Luckily, I didn't have to. Ang Moh Accent always pre-recorded the New Year's Eve wrap – an annual piece on the best places to catch the fireworks in Singapore – nice and early so he could finish his working year early.

I just went along to help Chain-Smoking Chinese Cameraman with the equipment. I didn't want to stay in the office and listen to the fake empathy around me.

At a Marina Bay Financial Centre bar, I ignored all the Christmas parties and held up a lighting reflector as Ang Moh Accent gushed over the view from the outdoor terrace. He knew the bar manager and had planned to bring a few friends down for New Year's Eve.

He noticed that I was distracted. He said, 'Eh, Millie, You OK or not. My lighting is awful.'

I mumbled something about the heat and noise.

Chain-Smoking Chinese Cameraman gazed lovingly at an ashtray and said, 'She's upset about that one. The gay one.'

Ang Moh Accent didn't even try to hide his disdain. He said, 'I told him so many times already. Cannot flaunt it.'

I said, 'Flaunt what? He just made a joke about an actor.'

Ang Moh Accent said, 'No. He was making a statement.'

'Exactly,' said Chain-Smoking Chinese Cameraman.

'Singapore knows it exists,' said Ang Moh Accent. 'But Singapore doesn't want to know it exists.'

'Exactly,' said Chain-Smoking Chinese Cameraman.

'Mr Louder knows the rules,' said Ang Moh Accent.

'Exactly,' said Chain-Smoking Chinese Cameraman.

I turned on my repetitive colleague and said, 'Is that all you can say?'

'I'm going for a smoke,' he said.

As Chain-Smoking Chinese Cameraman pulled the Marlboro from his breast pocket, Ang Moh Accent put a patronising hand on my shoulder. He said, 'It's good to be idealistic when you're young. I used to be like that.'

I wondered what had happened.

Ang Moh Accent seemed confused. 'Nothing happened,' he said. 'I grew up.'

An hour later, I received a WhatsApp message:

> *'Hey Monkey Girl. You don't like me, is it? Come and visit lah.'*

When I arrived at his hospital bedside, I was the only visitor. It was late, but not late enough to be left alone, not on Christmas Eve.

Mr Louder looked terrible. His face was pale and haggard. He was not in hospital with nervous exhaustion. I could see that. I could also see that there was no point in discussing it.

Mr Louder grimaced as he sat up in bed. He said, 'How do I look?'

'Not bad,' I said, trying not to focus on his wristband.

'Lying bitch,' he said.

I admitted that he looked like shit.

He liked that. He reached over for the water jug but couldn't quite reach. I stood up and poured him a glass. He grabbed it with shaky hands. He said, '*Wah*, you used to be my intern, now you're my mother, is it?'

I did feel older. *Wearier*.

I thought about my friends, doing their Masters, still hanging out in the same Jurong coffee shops, talking the same shit about government scholarships and career opportunities.

I thought about my first day as a news reporter, watching Peranakan Pervert ogle my breasts. I could just about picture myself sitting in his glassy office.

I was a child.

I said, 'Has your mother come?'

'Not yet,' he said, sipping his water. 'Maybe later.'

'What about Mr Loud?'

'No need. This hospital is not an official sponsor of the Rojak Breakfast Show.'

He made me laugh. He was always the funniest DJ. And the loudest. And the kindest. He had empathy for outsiders like me, which made sense. He had lived a life on the outside. Of all the people I'd met in the industry, he was the only one who wanted nothing from me.

Peranakan Pervert and Hokkien Half-Ball wanted to sleep with me to win a bet.

Slick Scholar just wanted to sleep with me.

Captain Mayhem wanted to flirt with me, in a dirty old man kind of way, and Mother Superior wanted to humiliate me.

Mr Louder was the exception. He just wanted to help because he could. And he was lying alone in a hospital bed.

So I talked nonsense for as long as possible. I made fun of Mr Loud's ego. I mocked Ang Moh Accent's vocal delivery. I did a terrible impression of Chain-Smoking Chinese Cameraman hunting down a pack of cigarettes. I did everything I could to distract us both from the real reason why Mr Louder was under hospital supervision. Eventually, he asked for my opinion. I told him he didn't need to ask. He knew how I felt.

He said, 'They suspended me for age-inappropriate content, Millie. I'm finished.'

I tried to brush off his concerns. But I didn't believe my words and nor did he.

He said, 'My family won't even visit. They won't bring their kids, my own nephews, because I'm age-inappropriate. What does age-inappropriate mean? They think I'm a paedophile, is it?'

'Of course not.'

'Then what am I, Millie?'

I held his hand and said, 'You are a terrible dancer at Heaven nightclub.'

He giggled as he cried. He asked me to keep him company for a little longer. I was supposed to have dinner with my family, but I wasn't going anywhere. I played silly Christmas songs on my phone and promised to stay until either another visitor showed up or he fell asleep.

I sat at his bedside until he fell asleep.

Day 145

I visited my friend in the hospital.

My Dad visited his friends in the KTV lounge.

Merry Christmas.

Day 148

The bosses have decided that a TV interview with Mr Louder might put an end to the incessant speculation. Rival news outlets had led with the story for days.

One of Mr Louder's second cousins had told a website that the DJ had always been a troubled soul, but the second cousin would continue to pray for that troubled soul.

Connected sources continued to claim that our newsroom was deeply unhappy with Mr Louder's suspension and wanted their colleague to return to the Rojak Breakfast Show.

In a short, terse email to staff, Captain Mayhem demanded to know who these so-called 'connected sources' were. Slick Scholar reminded him that there had been many retrenchments in the last year or so.

Captain Mayhem sent a second, polite email, thanking journalists for their hard work and asking us not to comment on Mr Louder's unfortunate situation.

Within an hour, connected sources had told rival news outlets that our journalists were being gagged.

Slick Scholar then told Captain Mayhem's secretary to delicately ask Captain Mayhem not to send any more emails.

Feeling ostracised, Captain Mayhem insisted that we go straight to the horse's mouth and speak to Mr Louder, who was still being paid a good salary not to work. Captain Mayhem wanted Ang Moh Accent to do the interview as he was the respected face of Singapore TV news. Surveys had shown that his western accent made him a more trustworthy figure.

But Ang Moh Accent was hosting a New Year's Eve party for a cryptocurrency firm at the Marina Bay Financial Centre.

Hokkien Half-Ball put Mr Loud's name forward, but Mr Loud highlighted the obvious conflict of interest (and he'd just signed a new radio contract and didn't want his reputation tarnished among those who might engage his public speaking services in the New Year).

Smooth Voice was the next choice, but he was on medical leave with chronic bronchitis.

Later, the inevitable phone call came. It was Slick Scholar. He said, 'You're doing the interview. Don't screw up.'

Day 149

I informed Mr Louder that he was being interviewed on New Year's Eve. No one else had.

Day 151

My friends headed to New Year's Eve parties all over town. I headed to an assignment I didn't want.

The interview took place at a swanky condo belonging to one of Mr Louder's friends. The friend wasn't around, but the absent owner had insisted on a strict no-smoking policy, which left me with a seriously pissed-off cameraman.

As Chain-Smoking Chinese Cameraman set up the tripod, I watched Mr Louder apply his own makeup. He said, 'Gotta hide the shitty bits, Millie.'

I said, 'You look good.'

He said, 'Wah, lucky you're pretty, Millie, because you're a lousy liar.'

Mr Louder was right. He appeared marginally better than when he was in hospital a few days ago, but he was certainly not ready for this. His eyes were puffy and bloodshot. He looked haunted. He applied extra foundation to his cheeks and examined himself in a compact mirror.

He muttered, 'So old already.'

His clothing choices didn't help. Normally, he looked like a fluorescent marker pen in the studio. His hair was dyed and his T-shirts were usually bright yellows and greens. His persona came in technicolour.

But he had muted himself. He sat on the sofa in white shirt and black trousers. He didn't have the body to pull off that combo. Slick Scholar dressed in the same way, but he had an athletic physique that gave him a magazine cover vibe. Mr Louder was middle-aged and flabby. He looked like he should be waving a Singapore flag at the National Day Parade.

I said, 'You joining the PAP, is it?'

He said, 'Balls *lah*, got to be conservative for this one. Trying to save my career.'

Chain-Smoking Chinese Camera Man signalled that he was ready to start. But I had to say something first. Something that had been eating away at me ever since Slick Scholar had ruined our bed talk with a warning.

I leaned over to check Mr Louder's lapel mic. There was nothing wrong with his mic, but I wanted to give my friend a shred of dignity. I whispered, 'We have to be careful about the gay thing.'

He said, 'What? You've told them all about our gay thing, Millie?'

He winked at Chain-Smoking Chinese Camera Man.

Mr Louder had switched on his flamboyant persona like a defensive shield. It just made me feel even shittier.

I said, 'Seriously. They don't want you to say it. Or they don't want you to promote it. You know. Cannot endorse it.'

I was rambling. For a moment, I thought that I might burst into tears. And then I thought that Mr Louder might do the same.

Instead, he did the strangest thing. He patted my hand and said, '*Aiyoh*, it's OK, Millie. We always know what to do.'

For the next half an hour or so, I watched a gay man not mention the word once.

I watched a gay man apologise for the 'inappropriate content' of suggesting another man was handsome.

I watched a gay man pretend to be anything other than a gay man.

Back at the office, the bosses had only praise for the interview footage. Captain Mayhem expected huge online viewing figures on New Year's Day. Slick Scholar praised my professionalism at the editors meeting. Even Hokkien Half-Ball mumbled something about a 'good job' as we passed each other awkwardly in the corridor.

Mother Superior approved the release of the video, but only after she expressed her discomfort at my use of the word 'gay'.

In one question, I had asked Mr Louder if the repeal of a law criminalising gay sex might change the way same-sex relationships are viewed in Singapore. Mr Louder had said he was not able to speak for an entire community. He had not condoned same-sex relationships.

But Mother Superior didn't like the juxtaposition of 'gay' and 'sex' in an interview between two employees for a family-friendly audience.

She said, 'It's a leading question that just makes me think of gay sex.'

Everything seemed to make her think of gay sex.

The woman was obsessed. But the question was cut.

The editors had protected thousands of innocent lives from the terror of juxtaposition.

After 11pm, I headed to The Float @ Marina Bay, where the New Year's Eve fireworks were going to be a multisensory feast for the senses.

We were also promised dazzling pyrotechnics and state-of-the-art light and sound technologies.

I know, because these were the descriptions that I was advised to lift from the press release.

PR companies can type this shit. But it's hard to say on camera.

The pre-fireworks New Year's Eve show was a bit like the National Day Parade, only shorter and cheaper. As a result, only two of the Four Major Races had been selected for hosting duties. There was the male Chinese Personality and the female Malay Artiste, which ticked most of the nation's boxes.

Chain-Smoking Chinese Camera Man and I watched from the side of the stage as the two hosts struggled to care. They were essentially keeping the live crowd awake until our TV broadcast went live from Marina Bay, just a few minutes before midnight. Chinese Personality instructed the drowsy audience to wave their glow-sticks and make some noise.

Malay Artiste told a few racy jokes.

Almost six months ago, I had raced around the National Day Parade like a wild-eyed rookie, chasing quotes and getting sunburned. Now, I was checking the time and checking in on Mr

Louder's welfare.

Just doing the job was making me feel guilty.

At 11.59pm, Chain-Smoking Chinese Camera Man captured the rowdy countdown and then the fireworks – AKA *artisanal fireworks*, according to the press release – and then panned across to me.

With a glittering, exploding Marina Bay skyline behind me, I smiled into the camera and said: 'Singaporeans cheered in the New Year with dazzling pyrotechnics that really were a multisensory feast for the senses.'

When we wrapped, Chain-Smoking Chinese Camera Man said: 'Bit random.'

I said, 'Yep. Don't care.'

At 12.15am, Slick Scholar called to check if Chain-Smoking Chinese Camera Man and I were still joining him and the other journalists for drinks.

Chain-Smoking Chinese Cameraman quickly said no. Slick Scholar pointed out that he was picking up the tab. Chain-Smoking Chinese Cameraman quickly said yes.

I waited for him to hurriedly pack away his equipment and then I called a taxi.

At 1am, Mr Louder and I toasted the New Year by getting drunk together in his friend's apartment.

Day 152

I woke up to a new year in a cold sweat and a strange place. A half-naked gay man was snoring on the floor beside me.

Mr Louder was wearing his boxer shorts and little else.

I was lying on the sofa, still wearing my crumpled clothes. The living room was stifling. We had obviously forgotten to switch on the air-conditioning.

The whisky seeped through my drenched pores. I sat up and grabbed my phone beside the empty glasses. The room temperature wasn't the only reason for my skin leaking.

As promised, my editors had released our interview online as an early New Year's present for a nosy nation.

The headline was pure clickbait: *Sorry DJ breaks his silence.*

But the video was surprisingly empathetic. Mr Louder came across as contrite (unnecessarily) but never apologised directly for what he was (correctly) and my self-conscious stammering had been edited out (luckily).

I sounded professional. Mr Louder sounded sincere.

On the living room floor, Mr Louder groaned and rolled over, coughing all over an expensive-looking rug. He asked how it was.

I said, 'Not bad, actually.' I meant it too.

Mr Louder sat up slowly and said, 'Yeah, I heard most of it. Maybe they'll have me back.'

He was fishing for early morning compliments.

'You know they will,' I said. 'The Rojak Breakfast Show has another ratings survey after Chinese New Year.'

'I wasn't talking about the bosses,' he said, far too softly.

I remembered we were alone in someone else's apartment. Mr Louder had nowhere else to go.

'The video has come out well,' I said.

Mr Louder seemed satisfied. He rose slowly to his feet and staggered towards the bathroom. I returned to my phone. 'Maybe don't read the comments,' I blurted out.

'Yeah, whatever *lah*. Happy New Year, Monkey Girl,' he said, scratching his ass as he closed the bathroom door behind him.

Day 153

My six-month probationary period was coming to an end so I decided to compile a quick list of work-related New Year's Resolutions:

I will push for more meaningful TV assignments.
I will not compromise my editorial output for commercial or political reasons.
I will eat a healthier diet and prepare more meals at home.
I will convince my parents that I can still have a viable career in local media.

Day 156

Spent three hours in a shopping mall today, getting vox pops about what prosperity means as Chinese New Year approaches.

I was assured that my assignment had nothing to do with the recent launch of the Prosperity Chicken Wrap, Prosperity Curly Fries and Prosperity Strawberry Shake or their extensive advertising campaigns across our media platforms.

I took an upsized prosperity meal home for dinner.

My mother said the *ang moh* junk food would make me fat.

My father said my TV piece was embarrassing and ate my Prosperity Curly Fries.

Day 161

Captain Mayhem called me into his office today. He thought my Chinese New Year clip on prosperity was 'cute' and the viewing figures were 'impressive'.

Then he rested his hands on his desk and turned serious. He said, 'Millie, all our newsrooms need to be revamped this year as we migrate over to online. We cannot stagnate. So, I've been hearing a lot about this ChatGPT.'

He leaned closer, almost conspiratorially and said, 'What is it?'

I said, 'How do you mean?'

The CEO of our media organisation checked no one was hovering outside his glass-walled office and said, 'My editors keep talking about it in meetings. What is it?'

I said, 'It's like a chatbot.'

Captain Mayhem's eyes suggested he didn't have a clue. 'Yah, go on,' he said.

'Well, I don't know that much. It's quite new tech,' I said. 'It's like A.I.'

Captain Mayhem perked up. 'Oh, I remember that show. I took my wife.'

I tried to explain that I wasn't referring to a movie, but to a chatbot that can answer questions and write essays and news reports.'

The CEO seemed impressed. He said, 'Yeah, Slick Scholar keeps saying it may revolutionise the media industry, especially for younger ones like you. What do you think, Millie?'

I wasn't sure what answer he was looking for. Clearly, my CEO wanted a serious response to a serious question. But I didn't know much about the chatbot myself, beyond some basic reading. So I decided to build an argument for what younger ones like me could do.

I told him that ChatGPT could not have written my first-person piece about the injured dancer at the National Day Parade.

A chatbot could not improvise the banter that the guys came up with every morning on the Rojak Breakfast Show.

And a chatbot could not have interviewed Mr Louder with such sensitivity.

I believed every word, but the fact that I'd spoken so passionately had clearly had an impact.

Captain Mayhem sat back in his leather executive chair and said, 'Wah, that was quite a speech, Millie.'

I suddenly felt very self-conscious. I said, 'Sorry, I got a bit carried away.'

He dismissed my apology with a wave and said, 'No, you're exactly right. Forget this ChatGPT nonsense. I want real human-interest stories from young reporters like you.'

I was immediately energised.

'And luckily,' he added, 'I've got one more monkey.'

Day 163

In the afternoon, I met Chain-Smoking Malay Cameraman at a remote petrol station off Mandai Road. The place was in an industrial estate beside the Mandai forest and Singapore Wildlife Sanctuary Group's eco-tourism project.

After Chain-Smoking Malay Cameraman was told off for trying to light up at a petrol station, I went off in search of my interviewee. I approached an elderly petrol pump attendant and said, 'Excuse me, have you seen a monkey?'

The old man pointed up at some rustling tree branches beside the petrol station and said, 'He only come down when car come.'

The petrol station was empty. So I pulled out my phone and watched the video clip again.

A driver had recently recorded a long-tailed macaque sitting on his car while he pumped petrol. When the driver was finished, the monkey leapt onto the roof of another car and observed the pumping process again, like an attendant. He jumped from car to car four times, watching each driver fill their tanks.

The video had been viewed more than a million times.

According to the comments, viewers were either rolling on the floor laughing or laughing their asses off. One commentator said that it was the 'FUNNIEST VIDEO EVER'.

It was a monkey sitting on a car roof. We really needed to get out more.

But Captain Mayhem was only interested in those million hits and wanted a piece to camera from me, preferably with the monkey doing his 'petrol pump attendant thing' behind me.

After an hour, I had counted more than a hundred cars. The bloody monkey never came down from his high branch once.

To pass the time, Chain-Smoking Malay Cameraman decided to stand beneath the tree and film some B-roll of the monkey snacking on some leaves.

The monkey peed on him.

I knew how the monkey felt.

At dusk, we gave up, called a taxi and left.

At 7.30pm, the petrol pump attendant sent me a text. The monkey had climbed down from the tree. I asked the taxi driver to return to the petrol station and ignored the bitching from Chain-Smoking Malay Cameraman.

At 7.35pm, the petrol pump attendant sent me an adorable video of the monkey leaping from one customer's roof to another. The bloody thing was toying with us.

At 7.45pm, we arrived back at the petrol station.

The monkey was dead.

According to the petrol pump attendant, the monkey had spotted a dropped fruit on the forecourt and helped himself.

But he didn't spot the truck heading for pump no. 2.

We recorded a short interview with the petrol pump attendant, who mentioned that monkeys had started hanging around to escape the construction of the Singapore Wildlife Sanctuary Group's eco-tourism project.

At 10pm, the clip was posted on our website. The line about the Singapore Wildlife Sanctuary Group was cut.

Day 165

Captain Mayhem called me up to his office again today. I could see that he was distracted. He didn't stare at my breasts.

His eyes darted all over the place. His conservative haircut normally looked like it was parted with a lawnmower, but his fringe was floppy and sweaty.

He turned his laptop around. My video was still among the most-viewed clips on our website, which clearly did not please him. He said, 'Your story about the monkey is getting negative feedback.'

I asked him why.

He said, 'The monkey is dead.'

I was aware of that. I had an O-Level in biology. But he was obviously distressed, so I highlighted the number of hits and the fact that I was the only one to get the story, which the other news outlets were now picking up, rewriting my content and trying to pass it off as their own.

My CEO was not easily pacified. He said, 'The content is free, on our TV channels and online. Of course it'll get hits. The advertisers are concerned.'

I said, 'Why? They didn't kill the monkey.'

My sarcasm was not appreciated. In fact, when the biggest boss in my media organisation began to turn a funny shade of purple, I realised that my lame joke was ill-judged.

Speaking through gritted teeth, Captain Mayhem said, 'I know they didn't literally kill the monkey, Millie. But our viewers will believe that they did. They are developing his home across the road.'

He wanted to know why we'd been unable to coax the monkey down from the tree with some food or something.

I told him that I was under the impression that we were not to interfere with wildlife and stage the filming of animals.

He shouted, 'You're not David Attenborough!'

His perspiring forehand had turned veiny. He pulled a handkerchief from his pocket and wiped his face.

I said, 'I know that, but it was only a gimmicky story, a follow-up on a TikTok video.'

He slapped his hands against the table and said, 'Exactly, and they're killing us. Every million views for them is a million views taken from us. In banking, it was just bank against bank. Here, it's us against five million camera phones. How to compete? We're supposed to be the respected voice of Singapore media, Millie.'

In that case, I asked, why was I being sent to report on a jumping monkey?

Our CEO said, 'Because that's what our audience wants, jumping monkeys.'

Day 166

After a lousy day feeling sorry for myself (and the dead monkey), I went to bed with Slick Scholar, who decided to mansplain the media business to me.

According to him, Captain Mayhem was right.

Lying beside me, he said, 'We're just too small and too conservative to have bleeding heart liberals running around for a week to do a feature on green washing. We don't have the staff or the budget for that stuff, not anymore. We're an industry in terminal decline. We just have to pick battles that we can win.'

He rolled onto his side and eyed my chest.

I said, 'Yeah, they're not a battle you can win tonight.'

He giggled and said, 'What? I like a challenge.'

I pulled the duvet up to my shoulders. His flirting wasn't working.

I said, 'I'm not stupid. I don't expect to do award-winning stuff every day.'

He said, 'You just didn't expect so many jumping monkeys.'

'Dead monkeys,' I corrected. 'If it was still a jumping monkey, your sex talk might work.'

'Bastard monkey,' said Slick Scholar.

He gave up trying to grope my breasts and sat up against the headboard. His abs still looked impressive.

He said, 'OK, get it off your chest. Pun completely intended.'

I sat up with him, keeping the duvet pulled up to my neck. I needed him to concentrate.

I recounted my ridiculous meeting with Captain Mayhem

again and the pointless chase for social media numbers. I said, 'We're supposed to lead the news coverage. Now we just follow it.'

Slick Scholar straightened the duvet across his legs. He was always neat and meticulous, even in bed. He said, 'That sounds like an NTU line. Did you hear that in NTU?'

'Can't remember,' I lied. Our tutors often rambled on about leading the news coverage, rather than following it.

Slick Scholar grinned at me and said, 'Yes you can. I know all the tutors on your course. Most of them couldn't hack it full-time. Those who can, do; those who can't, teach idealistic Mass Comm students about the virtues of pure reporting. And they're right, until they work with politicians who want to sign off on every press release. Or advertisers who demand everything or take their money to Facebook. Or readers who whack us every day for being government lackeys. So what do we do? Give up? No *lah*. We pick our battles. We send you to do the monkey shit to get hits online. OK. Fine. And then, we can slip you in to interview Mr Louder, because we know you'll do a gentle piece that'll do more for gay rights than a dozen Pink Dot Parades.'

I frowned at his cynicism.

He said, 'Don't look at me like that. You know I'm right. Does a thousand pink T-shirts change a nation's thinking and a government policy? No. We do. We're the barometers for the public. We test the water for the government. We know exactly where the OB markers are and that's how we move them. We get things changed, at society's pace, not mine and not yours, whether we like it or not. It's a game, but we still play it better than anyone else. And that's why we'll outlast them all.'

Without thinking, I started rolling back the duvet and said, 'Nice speech. I like smart men.'

He leaned towards me and said, 'Yeah? I like smart women.'

We both laughed at our lousy dialogue and kicked the duvet to the floor. Honestly, I wasn't so bothered about the dead monkey anymore.

Day 167

The sex must have been good last night because I woke up late for work. I was so tired that I mistyped my email password three times and was locked out of my account.

Our media company takes its privacy and security very seriously.

To reset my password, I needed to call Chirpy IT Uncle. He's a lovely Indian man who lives for his modified keyboards and panic-stricken calls from journalists.

Chirpy IT Uncle asked me to set a new password with upper and lowercase letters, numbers and a special character. He said, 'Security is no joke, OK?'

Then I had to download an app to my phone to enable two-factor authentication. Then I had to generate a code on the app and type it into my email account to authenticate my new password.

Then I couldn't remember the sequence of upper and lowercase letters, numbers and special characters and failed three password attempts and had to repeat the process.

Finally, I got into my account and read an internal email about the latest round of retrenchments. Chirpy IT Uncle and I had no idea which departments might be affected.

Luckily, the news had already been leaked to rival media organisations, who had kindly listed all the affected departments.

Our media company takes its privacy and security very seriously.

After lunch, Lauren asked to see me on the news floor. In the past, she would've just wandered down to the TV floor for a chat. But our relationship had been a bit frosty since she'd told me about Hokkien Half-Ball and her promotion.

Beckoning me to her desk was her petty power play. She was a lifestyle deputy editor. I was still on probation. And she was mostly pissed off these days.

In fact, she barely looked up from her laptop. She said, 'I'm doing a piece on the best lion dances over Chinese New Year. Slick Scholar said he's asked you to do something.'

I told her that I was getting some vox pops and B-roll for Ang Moh Accent's round-up of the major events. I wasn't even going to be on camera. I was hardly ending my TV training stint with a bang.

Lauren said, 'I just wanna make sure there's no overlap.'

I leaned over her cubicle and said, 'I haven't done anything wrong, Lauren.'

'Yeah, OK,' she sighed.

'But I haven't,' I insisted.

She leaned back in her chair and checked no one else was eavesdropping. But no one was. The news floor was like the TV floor, which was also like the radio floor. They were mostly empty.

When I watched those inspirational media movies in NTU classes, the newsrooms were filled with American actors running around desks filled with papers and smoking sub-editors, racing to get their scoops onto page one before deadline.

Lauren and I were making sure that we didn't duplicate the same coverage of a lion dance.

The Pulitzer Price seemed further away than ever.

I insisted again that I hadn't done anything wrong. I liked Lauren. I didn't want her disliking me. She had been a kind of newsroom *jie jie* since my first day.

'Yeah, I know,' she said. 'It's just been a bit shitty lately. Self-esteem stuff.'

She pretended to check an email in her inbox. And I pretended to check a WhatsApp message on my phone. I didn't know what to say.

Just as I didn't know what to say when an angry face thundered towards us.

Just as I didn't know what to say when the angry face turned into a slightly familiar face.

Just as I didn't know what to do when I felt myself being brushed aside.

The slightly familiar face said, 'Eh, you cannot be discreet, is it?'

The slap was hard. I felt the burning sting from a distance. Lauren's face jolted backwards. Her head clipped the side of her cubicle.

The slightly familiar face turned to me and said, 'At least you were discreet.'

She was no longer a slightly familiar face. She was the innocent face at the Family Fun Day. She was the Madonna and Child, smiling together, waiting for husband and father to return.

She was Hokkien Half-Ball's wife.

My first, puerile thought was to reflect on her doll-like beauty. She was the classic girl next door, the demure Asian with minimal makeup and a wholesome smile. She was blessed with that natural sweetness that wins starring roles on Chinese soap operas and attracts men who fantasise over anime characters in school uniforms. She was going to be the perfect mother and wife in the Confucian sense, submitting to all the men in her family.

Until Lauren and I came along.

I felt sorry for her, but only to a point. I hadn't knowingly disrespected her – I hadn't even known of her existence until the Family Fun Day – but I was aware of the gathering eyeballs on the news floor. So I said, 'Excuse me, I wasn't being discreet. I didn't know that Hokkien Half-Ball was married.'

She said, 'I know *lah*. But this one knew. This one knew and she told the whole fucking world. I got kids, you bitch.'

Hokkien Half-Ball's wife went for Lauren's hair and yanked hard. Lauren screamed like a pig and then used her own hair to pull Hokkien Half-Ball's wife towards her. The pain must have been unbearable, but her primal instincts had kicked in. Lauren slapped Hokkien Half-Ball's Wife across the cheek, which freed her hair at least. The two of them then grabbed each other in a headlock and tumbled to the carpet.

Hokkien Half-Ball Wife's said, 'You're a slut.'

The comment only provoked Lauren. She screamed, 'I'm not a fucking slut.' And then she went for the long, silky hair of

Hokkien Half-Ball's Wife.

Lauren screamed, 'Don't call me a fucking slut.'

When they started kicking each other's shins, I jumped between them, which made them accidentally kick my shins. I yelped like a puppy and jumped aside.

The two of them were nose-to-nose at this point.

I went in again and led with my hands, as if I was diving into a swimming pool. I pushed my fingertips between their noses and wrenched their faces apart. One of them accidentally scratched the back of my hand. I grabbed Lauren under the armpits and dragged her away from Hokkien Half-Ball's Wife. The pair were still lashing out when other journalists finally decided to stop gawking and intervened to separate them.

Lauren and Hokkien Half-Ball Wife's continued to circle each other, but there were too many bodies between them now. We were all breathing heavily and shaking. The back of my hand was bleeding. Lauren's face was red and swollen. Hokkien Half-Ball's Wife was crying.

Eventually, Slick Scholar came storming through the labyrinth of cubicles. I had never seen him like this before. He was raging. 'You three, in my office, now,' he shouted.

I kept the warring women apart as Slick Scholar led us away.

Hokkien Half-Ball's Wife called Lauren a cheap slut for shagging her husband.

Lauren called Hokkien Half-Ball Wife's a hypocritical slut for staying with her husband.

Hokkien Half-Ball was hiding in the toilet.

Slick Scholar was amazing in his office. He had calmed down and taken stock of the situation within seconds of closing the door. His voice was measured. He was reasoning with a clear head. This is what an all-boys elite school education really gives Singaporean men. It's not just a quiet authority to lead. Slick Scholar has always had that. It's the unshakeable belief that such men are the only ones in the room capable of leading with a quiet authority.

Watching Slick Scholar work each woman in his office was like watching an audition, not just for Captain Mayhem's job, but for parliament. His smooth bullshit would work wonders around the coffee shops of his future constituency on a sweaty Sunday morning.

And he was bilingual. And he was handsome. And he was mostly compliant. He was almost too good to be true.

Slick Scholar assured Lauren that the matter should remain in-house as she was a rising star in the newsroom. She agreed. Apparently, there were some photos on Instagram. Lauren's mother wasn't on Instagram and not aware of the affair. Lauren hoped to keep it that way.

Slick Scholar assured me that the matter should remain in-house because I was building a name for myself as a versatile reporter across all media platforms. I was inclined to agree. I was still on probation.

Slick Scholar assured Hokkien Half-Ball's wife that the matter should remain in-house because he empathised with her potential loss of face. She also agreed. She was in the process of organising a reunion dinner with all her aunties.

Slick Scholar then assured all of us that he would deal with Hokkien Half-Ball, once Hokkien Half-Ball had finished in the toilet.

Day 168

My sleep was horrendous last night. I had this recurring dream. Hokkien Half-Ball was hosting a live gameshow from a Singapore Pools outlet. He had oily hair and was dressed in a garish red and gold jacket. He looked like a human *hong bao*.

Lauren, Hokkien Half-Ball's Wife and I were the contestants. We were all dressed in white and asked questions about his sex life. If we answered correctly, we were allowed to move a step closer to a grinning Hokkien Half-Ball. If we answered wrongly, the other two contestants were allowed to slap our faces.

We stood in front of a wall filled with TV screens, displaying our latest odds of winning. The studio audience was a sea of glowing handphones in the darkness, filming every answer.

It was never revealed what we were playing for. The prize was a mystery.

But it didn't matter. I never got a single question right. I had the same answer for everything.

At one point, Hokkien Half-Ball asked the contestants to describe his favourite position. I buzzed in and said, 'Batam!'

'Incorrect,' he said.

Then he asked the contestants what he liked to do immediately after waking up. I buzzed in again and said, 'Batam!'

'Incorrect,' he said gleefully.

In the studio audience, my father applauded loudly.

Day 169

Slick Scholar had wisely given Lauren and me the day off. Hokkien Half-Ball was going to be given the day off, too, but the Singapore Budget was coming up. The editors had to utilise their best resources.

I messaged Lauren to meet for lunch. We needed to clear the air. She took half an hour to reply. 'Not near the office,' she said.

We met at a quiet café off Serangoon Road. It was central enough to be convenient, but quiet enough to be discreet.

Lauren looked as bad as I did. We both ordered double espressos and waited in silence for the barista. He was a poly student and flirty. We were neither and not in the mood.

We sat at the back of the café, away from the entrance.

Lauren mostly stared at her double espresso so I rambled on like an idiot, saying how Hokkien Half-Ball deserved everything, how lousy my sleep had been and how weird my dream was, which provoked a reaction.

Lauren looked up and said, 'We were in a contest? Who won?'

I said: 'No one. There wasn't even a prize.'

Lauren smirked and whispered, 'No *lah*, got punishment only.'

I insisted that the issue would blow over. The Instagram photos were an innocent mistake.

Lauren looked at me like I was stupid. She said, 'What mistake? I posted the photos of us deliberately. I wanted her to see us.'

I was incredulous. 'Why?'

'Because I was sick of being the "outside" woman,' she snapped. 'That's what she called me.'

'His wife?' I asked.

Lauren found my naivety annoying. She said, 'Of course. I don't know if she knew about you, but she definitely knew about me. Apparently, he came home one night and she said his clothes *smelled* of me. But it was OK. They had a long conversation, like grown-ups. And she just said his outside life cannot come inside. That's me. His outside life. The grown-ups had decided that I was allowed to be his outside fuck toy.'

Luckily, the café was quiet. Lauren's voice was rising.

I said, 'Come on ah. Don't say it like that. Like you said before, it's just a bit of fun, right?'

She said it wasn't fun. It was revenge for her and Hokkien Half-Ball.

'Against you,' she said.

I felt the sudden blast of the café's air-conditioning. I was shivering. I asked why, but the question felt like one for a government minister.

I knew the answer in advance.

Lauren said, 'You got him into a big fight with his wife and Slick Scholar, when you told HR what happened to you. He was mostly annoyed about Slick Scholar. And then later on, we got drunk at some media drinks event. He flirted with me, made me feel sorry for him. I was lonely and fed-up. And jealous.'

'Of me?' I asked. 'I was shagging a married man and no one told me. I was humiliated. Jealous of what?'

'Of him,' whispered Lauren.

'Oh yeah, he's such a catch. Gambles on football. Gambles on women. He's OK *lah*, but he's not Henry Golding.'

'Not him, the other one,' said Lauren, refusing to look at me.

Finally, I got the picture. Not Hokkien Half-Ball, obviously, but the one who looked like Henry Golding in his black trousers and immaculate white shirt.

'Ah, so you know, ah,' I said.

Now it was my turn to look down at the coffee.

'Please *lah*, everyone knows,' Lauren said. 'We can see you both in the meetings, like JC students. He gives you all the best assignments. Gave you the interview with Mr Louder. Gave you the Hollywood actor interview.'

Surprisingly, I felt my anger rising. I said, 'I got that Mr Louder interview because I worked with him on the breakfast show and because he asked me and because I might be good at my job.'

Lauren snapped right back at me. She said, 'No, you're *very* good. You must be the best. Because I also got promoted because of you.'

I asked her what the hell she was going on about.

She said, 'He dumped me for you. He gave me the promotion because of you. To keep me quiet. So how do you think I feel now, ah? I got dumped because he preferred me to you. And I also got promoted because he preferred me to you. Nice, right?'

I thought I'd been punched in the chest. Eventually, I mumbled, 'Slick Scholar?'

She said, 'Wah, you really are a good journalist.'

As my mind raced, I tried some mental arithmetic. Lauren was promoted around the time Slick Scholar and I started seeing each other. Her mood certainly changed towards me around that time, too. Stupidly, I'd put her attitude down to Hokkien Half-Ball's rebound fling with her. How was I supposed to know that it was Lauren having a rebound fling with him? The dates made sense, but nothing else did.

I asked her why she hadn't said anything.

She said, 'I don't know. You seemed happy and *so* clueless. I thought you'd work it out for yourself. And when you didn't … Actually, I kinda felt sorry for you.'

I felt like a naïve, bratty, stupid child.

I said, 'But you could've complained to upper management, like I did.'

'Complain about what?' She asked. 'Slick Scholar dumping me? Me getting a promotion? Me being upset that my ex-boyfriend is now going out with my friend? What can I say to HR? Anyway, I didn't want to say anything about you. You were nice to me.'

Now I really felt shitty. I asked if she wanted me to do anything.

'Like what? No need,' she said. 'You still got to finish your probation. I've finished with Hokkien Half-Ball and I've taken down the Instagram photos. That's it.'

I still felt compelled to speak up to HR or Captain Mayhem or someone.

She smiled at her espresso and said, 'Cannot. Just keep quiet and we are good girls. Complain and we are sluts. I don't want my Mum thinking that I'm a slut.'

When I got home, my Mum was chopping vegetables in the kitchen. She was humming along to the radio. The ballads were in English and she hardly knew the words, but she was addicted to those love song melodies.

I joined her at the table and silently passed her the cabbage. Without looking up from her chopping board, she said in Mandarin, 'You're late.'

'Long day,' I replied in English.

We often communicated this way. She knew enough English to understand and my Mandarin was good enough for the kitchen table, but we often reverted to this bilingual conversation, almost as a point of principle.

I realised we were alone. Again. I asked where Dad was.

'Batam,' she whispered.

I said, 'Oh, another business trip, is it?'

My petulant sarcasm interrupted her chopping. She looked me up and down and said, 'Nice top. Pretty.'

I said, 'But I look fat, right?'

She shook her head and said, 'No. You look pretty.'

Mum returned to her vegetable chopping. She smiled at the company suddenly joining us in the kitchen. Smooth Voice was back on the radio, preparing another ballad for his devoted housewives.

Day 170

Overslept this morning. Didn't care. I only had three jobs to complete today.

Help Ang Moh Accent edit his Chinese New Year package.

Fill in my appraisal form for HR before the Chinese New Year break.

Confront Slick Scholar.

At 10am, I staggered into the editing studio. Ang Moh Accent boosted my self-esteem by saying my straggly hair was a mess and my makeup was all over the place.

I reminded him that I wasn't scheduled to go on camera today. He reminded me that he always wore his on-camera attire just in case he gets called out in an emergency. I reminded him that he wasn't a fireman.

As he edited my footage, he tutted under his breath and muttered something about my delivery. Apparently, I sounded 'too Singlish at times'.

I told him that he sounded 'too Downton Abbey at times'.

He pointed out that his received pronunciation ensured he was understood with a multiracial, multilingual audience.

I said, 'That's why you sound like a British butler, is it?'

He suggested that I grab a coffee to 'wake up a bit'. Then he could edit the video in peace and prepare his feedback for my two-month probationary stint in TV. He was not subtle. But he was right.

I apologised for being so bitchy. I explained that I had personal and professional issues to deal with, which were serious, but no excuse.

Ang Moh Accent nodded and said, 'Yeah, I heard about Hokkien Half-Ball's Wife. Must have been really awkward.'

To be honest, I'd forgotten about Hokkien Half-Ball's Wife. That was twenty-four hours and two dodgy boyfriends ago.

I bought a coffee, but the caffeine had no impact on my shaking hands. Sitting alone in the staff canteen, I had this strange epiphany.

I was terrified.

It made perfect sense that I was terrified. I had plenty of reasons to be terrified. But I watched my hands shake at the table and realised, for the first time, that I'd never felt like this before.

I'm not a control freak – at least I don't think I am – but my life has been freakishly controlled.

My intellect got me into an elite, all-girls Catholic school.

My exam results got me onto the Mass Comm course at NTU. My NTU performance got me a media scholarship.

My scholarship got me fast-tracked through one of Asia's leading media companies. And my naïve sex life at one of Asia's leading media companies got me here.

Sitting alone. Shaking.

Being terrified was a weird sensation because I couldn't control it. I just *was*.

I was powerless to my own emotions, which was annoying because I didn't think terror was the right choice. Why terror? What was I terrified of? What had I done wrong? I'd slept with two colleagues – both of whom I assumed were single at the time – and the relationships were consensual.

I should've felt silly, or irritated, or embarrassed, but not terrified. Being terrified felt wrong or weak.

Because I knew why. Deep down. I was terrified of the repercussions. My job. My rice bowl. My parents. My shame. Were they good enough reasons to be terrified? It didn't matter.

It was my reality.

I was one day away from a guaranteed confirmation as a journalist, the only thing I'd ever wanted since I'd designed newspaper pages in secondary school art class.

But that wasn't the real reason either. Lauren had spelled it out for me yesterday.

Keep quiet and we are good girls. Complain and we are sluts.

Lauren was not a slut. And nor was I. Lauren was a recently promoted lifestyle deputy editor and I was still on probation. For one more day.

We were not sluts.

At 11am, I filled out my self-evaluation form for HR. The feedback from myself and my immediate supervisors would be compiled and discussed at my final appraisal meeting tomorrow.

My online news supervisor was Peranakan Pervert, who had left the company after blackmailing me to have sex with him. I refused. He was retrenched.

My radio supervisor was Smooth Voice, who had made me a trainee producer with Mr Loud and Mr Louder. The latter was hospitalised after his homosexuality was effectively considered 'inappropriate content'.

And my TV supervisor, in a literal sense, was Ang Moh Accent. I'd just irritated him by calling him a British butler.

But my real supervisor was Slick Scholar. I was having sex with him, but only after he'd sneakily dumped my friend for me.

I was going to ace my final appraisal, wasn't I?

Without thinking, I hammered away at the laptop. Everything and everyone was brilliant. My stints at news, radio and TV were all brilliant. The supervisors were all brilliant. The meetings were brilliant. The beanbags and coffee were brilliant. My workplace was a dream of technicolour brilliance.

How could it possibly be anything else? I was still on probation.

I was not a slut.

At 2pm, Slick Scholar gave me a playful grope in the corridor and waffled on about women in long trousers. He loved me in long trousers. I looked like an executive, apparently.

He checked there was no one else around and tried to kiss me, like a kid in the school playground. I shoved my hands in my pockets and pulled back.

He asked if there was anything wrong. It was almost funny, watching his enormous brain trying to explain an inexplicable reaction. There was no reason for me to pull away. I was still on probation. And he was my media hero. My boss.

I told him I was fine. Everything was awesome. I'd just finished editing our Chinese New Year TV package. My self-evaluation form was done. A glowing appraisal was on the way. My confirmation was pretty much inevitable. I was totally fine.

He wasn't convinced. He felt that I wasn't my usual self.

I said, 'Who am I then? Lauren?'

Now it was his turn to pull away. I didn't say anything else. I didn't need to. I was angry and Slick Scholar was smart.

He nodded and said, 'I thought she might tell you, after what happened.'

I said, 'After what happened? After she was humiliated by Hokkien Half-Ball's Wife? Or after she was humiliated by you?'

He acknowledged that both incidents might have had a

bearing on her mood. He insisted that the situation wasn't what it looked like.

He said, 'I'm not like them. Lauren and I had fun, but this is different.' He gestured at the space between us.

I said, 'Oh, this is real love, is it? In six months, there was Peranakan Pervert, Hokkien Half-Ball and you. All real love, is it? Or is it just the bosses fucking all the young reporters?'

'It's not like that,' he said softly. 'I didn't love Lauren. That's what she's angry about.'

'So you promoted her,' I said.

'Only on merit. OK, I felt lousy. The promotion was the least I could do,' he said.

Slick Scholar registered my shock. He said, 'Yeah, that came out wrong. I didn't promote her to make her feel better. I did it because I felt so bad.'

I said, 'Oh, so even her promotion is about you, is it? You keep her quiet and you get to feel better. And then you get me on top? Extra bonus.'

He threw his hands in the air and said, 'What do you want me to say, Millie? This is a workplace with intelligent, young people. Men and women meet in workplaces. They pair up. They stay together. Or they split up and move on.'

I said, 'But you promoted Lauren and gave me the best assignments.'

He said, 'You were both good.'

'In what way?' I asked.

An aircon technician interrupted us. Slick Scholar and I stood in silence, peering down at the carpet until the technician passed.

'Well?' I asked. 'Did we get those jobs on merit?'

Slick Scholar was adamant that I was the best young reporter he'd ever seen in the newsroom. I asked about Lauren.

He said, 'Yeah, sure, she would've got there eventually. And with the promotion, she had Hokkien Half-Ball to supervise her and, you know ...'

'You were both safe,' I sighed. 'I should tell her.'

Slick Scholar put an arm across my shoulder. I was too weary to resist. But I didn't reciprocate. That was my petty defiance. I kept my hands in my trouser pockets.

He said, 'What would it achieve? You'll humiliate her and lose a friend. And she'll go public. You saw what she did to Hokkien Half-Ball's poor family on Instagram. She ruined them. She's not like you. She's fragile. And questions will be asked about her, about you, about us, about the newsroom. For what? To make her feel better? It won't. How many careers would it ruin? Hers? Mine? Yours?'

I said, 'Why mine?'

He said, 'Well, you did get those assignments on merit. You really did. But they won't say that outside. They'll say you and Lauren just benefited from this ... I don't know ... this patriarchal culture.'

He laughed sarcastically because he knew he was right. If Lauren and I stayed quiet, we were journalists. If we complained, we were something else entirely.

Slick Scholar checked that we were still alone in the corridor and embraced me. He held me close to his chest. I felt his heartbeat coming through his swollen pec. The beat was slow and steady.

He said, 'Look, your confirmation is a formality. We all know that. But Captain Mayhem wants to get all the staff together in the newsroom tomorrow for *lo hei*. He might have a surprise for you.'

I didn't want a surprise from the CEO. I wasn't sure what I wanted anymore.

Day 172

FINAL APPRAISAL DAY

Our Chinese New Year package went out on TV today. Ang Moh Accent dominated the coverage, naturally. I popped up in a brief cameo to list the best lion dance performances in Singapore. It was nothing special, but Slick Scholar had still selected my clip to be cut for TikTok and Instagram.

According to Slick Scholar in the editors meeting, I appealed to the younger demographic that they were all desperately seeking on media platforms with short-attention spans.

According to Ang Moh Accent in the TV studio, I must be really good in bed.

I didn't even have the heart to retaliate. No bitchy reply. Nothing. I was walking around the building in a daze. I felt worthless. Empty. I had no fight left.

I watched the Chinese New Year package over and over again until I could no longer judge my performance objectively. Did my face really fit? Was I any good? Or was I sleeping with the man who made the editorial decisions? Objectivity was impossible now. I just wanted to run to the toilet and curl up in a ball. I wanted to be at home, sitting at the kitchen table, listening to Smooth Voice's love songs.

I wanted to feel legitimately wanted.

As expected, the appraisal was conducted on autopilot. Slick Scholar, Smooth Voice, Ang Moh Accent and an unsmiling woman from HR attended the meeting. They were all in a hurry to head off for their Chinese New Year gatherings.

Of course, Slick Scholar had another reason to slither away as soon as possible. Two of my original supervisors were absent, because I'd slept with one and refused to sleep with the other. I could feel HR Woman's eyes judging me.

She said, 'Hokkien Half-Ball is at a marketing meeting, but he's ticked all the right boxes for you on the news side. Anything to add, Smooth Voice?'

The radio station director coughed several times, swallowed the nicotine-drenched phlegm at the back of his throat and said, 'Yeah, good. Millie was good on the Rojak Breakfast Show. We only had one incident.'

HR Woman checked her notes and said, 'The durian thing?'

'No *lah*, that one not Millie's fault,' said Smooth Voice. 'I was talking about the Mr Louder thing. Actually, that one not her fault either. She wasn't working on the show at that time. But she did a nice piece on Mr Louder. It was good.'

HR Woman returned to her notes and picked out some of my achievements. She mentioned my first scoop with the injured dancer at the National Day Parade, the Mr Louder interview again and my monkey scoops.

She said, 'Yeah, you did a lot of stories on monkeys. You like monkeys, is it?'

I said, 'Only when they don't die.'

HR Woman looked strained. Slick Scholar managed a fake laugh. Smooth Voice tapped the cigarette packet, protruding from his jeans pocket. He seemed as bored as I was.

HR woman turned to her boss. She said, 'And what about TV?'

And of course, Slick Scholar went completely over the top. According to him, I sparkled in front of a camera. I made my interviewees feel comfortable. I lured them into giving me the best soundbites. My clips always performed well on YouTube. I still found time to interview Mr Louder in a mature and empathetic manner. I was the easiest confirmation he could remember. I was going to be such an asset as the company completed its evolution in the digital age.

HR Woman checked her watch. She had probably heard the rumours and wanted to get this grubby business over with. But she still had to get through the formalities first.

She said, 'There's nothing more to say then, Millie. We'll sort out the paperwork. I'm sure the editors will discuss where they'd like to assign you in the next few days. But that's about it for now. Your probation is done. Congratulations, Millie. You're a full-time journalist.'

HR Woman then asked if I had anything to add.

I said, 'Yeah. I quit.'

At 6pm, Captain Mayhem gathered every staff member in the newsroom. He was disappointed with the low turnout. He asked Mother Superior where everybody was. She reminded the CEO that many had gone away for Chinese New Year.

And she also whispered something about a recent retrenchment exercise.

Captain Mayhem moved on quickly and enthusiastically asked us to snuggle together and pick up chopsticks. His secretary had already prepared the ingredients on the table.

Captain Mayhem sprinkled the sauces onto the strips of raw fish and said, 'I asked my banking staff to do *lo hei* with me every year. Always brought us good luck. I hope this will do the same for us.'

I hoped he was right. Uncle Groper's chair was still empty.

Part of me felt sorry for Captain Mayhem. He was an old, successful businessman in the wrong industry. He didn't notice the eye-rolling or the sarcastic muttering. The head of Singapore's largest media organisation wasn't being heard. He was like a grandfather trying to understand the latest video game. His enthusiasm was almost heart-breaking. He kept calling on the journalists to gather closer, to grab chopsticks and share his excitement for the new year ahead.

But my colleagues didn't see such optimism. They saw a dwindling audience and empty chairs in the office. They were doing more for less. Every day. Tossing some shredded vegetables wasn't going to change that.

Captain Mayhem said, 'Come on *ah*, is everyone ready? Got some big announcements to make after this.'

I stood at the back and was eager to stay there. Captain Mayhem had done nothing wrong, not to me anyway. There had been the off-colour remarks about my appearance and the usual glances below my neck, but nothing I hadn't dealt with since university.

Still, he caught my eye. He said, 'Eh, Millie, there you are. Come to the front. Big confirmation day for you today. Everybody, Millie was confirmed today.'

The applause was polite, at best. Rumours spread quickly in a newsroom. I was involved in the grubby business with Hokkien Half-Ball's Wife. I was guilty by association.

Reluctantly, I made my way through the crowd when Slick Scholar appeared at my side, out of nowhere, grabbing my arm. Under his breath, he said, 'Don't do it.'

I said, 'Don't do what?'

Slick Scholar insisted that I knew what he was talking about, that I was about to throw us all under the bus, that I was about to sacrifice a promising career in the media, that I was going to miss out on so many opportunities in the digital age. He reminded me that I was comfortable in front of a laptop, a TV camera and even a radio mic. I had the tools for all facets of modern media.

I had everything, apparently, but I was about to throw it all away, for nothing.

I said, 'Why did you do it?'

Slick Scholar was confused. 'Do what?'

'Sleep with Lauren. Then dump Lauren to sleep with me. Then promote Lauren to keep sleeping with me. Why did you do all that?'

Slick Scholar shrugged and said, 'I liked you. I still do.'

I said, 'So it is about you. You get whatever you want from us, whenever you like.'

I tried to brush him off, but he pulled me to the side of the crowd, out of earshot of the others.

Captain Mayhem spotted us. Above the *lo hei* noise, he shouted, 'Eh, Millie, Slick Scholar, come and join us.'

Slick Scholar said, 'Hang on ah, just got to discuss a last-minute assignment.'

Captain Mayhem shook his head. 'That one ah. Never stops.'

He appeared to admire our work ethic. No one else in the room did. They had probably heard the rumours and made up their minds already.

Slick Scholar was still holding my arm. He said, 'You can't quit. Whatever reason you give, they won't believe it. And you can't tell the truth.'

He caught me off guard.

'Why?' I asked.

Slick Scholar almost smiled. He said, 'Come on ah, the media is so small here. For you and Lauren. Everyone would know in five minutes. You know what people will say about you. You wanna do that to Lauren?'

I said, 'I'm not doing it to Lauren. I'm doing it to you.'

I reached into my pockets. I was wearing the kind of trousers that made me look like a powerful female executive. The kind of trousers that Slick Scholar always liked.

The kind of trousers that came with deep pockets.

The kind of deep pockets that kept an iPhone discreetly concealed.

I hit the play button and savoured Slick Scholar's horror.

He heard himself say:

'What would it achieve? You'll humiliate her and lose a friend. And she'll go public. You saw what she did to

Hokkien Half-Ball's poor family on Instagram. She ruined them. She's not like you. She's fragile. And questions will be asked about her, about you, about us, about the newsroom. For what? To make her feel better? It won't. How many careers would it ruin? Hers? Mine? Yours?'

He heard himself condemn himself. He heard his passive-aggressive threat. He heard the entitlement, the certainty, dripping through his voice. He heard a career path crumbling.

Instinctively, he reached out for my phone. But I slipped it back into my pocket and said, 'It's on Google Docs. It's saved on my laptop. I even emailed it to myself.'

I had pulled off a miracle. Slick Scholar was speechless. The debating champion of his elite school couldn't string a sentence together, couldn't form words. He was impotent.

So I did the talking. I said, 'OK, I won't say anything about Lauren and nor will you. Her job and promotion are protected. No need for her to know what you did. And you'll give me a fantastic reference. It'll be an honest reference, right? And you'll tell Captain Mayhem and HR that I'm leaving for personal reasons. I got a sick Dad or something, which is kinda true. When other companies come to you for references, you'll be fair. And you can settle my scholarship bond. You know everyone right? Do all of that and we're fine. If you don't, I'll write out the whole thing for a blog or something.'

Slick Scholar took a moment to respond. He was clearly using that *atas* brain to work out what alternatives he had. Eventually, the debating champion of his elite school realised there was only one winning argument.

Mine.

'Yeah, OK,' he muttered.

I nodded and tried to make my way towards the noisy *lo hei* tossing. Slick Scholar pulled me back again. He said, 'Why are you doing this?'

It was a good, philosophical question, actually.

I thought about Lauren, struggling with her 'self-esteem stuff'.

I thought about my mother, chopping vegetables in the early hours.

And I thought about Hokkien Half-Ball and Peranakan Pervert giggling together in the news conferences. Placing bets. On me.

I said, 'Because you fuckers always win.'

Slick Scholar finally released his grip on my arm. He will never be allowed to touch me again. But he still had time for a sneering parting shot though.

He said, 'You know what you are, right?'

I said, 'Of course *lah*. I'm a journalist.'

I made my way through the crowd and stood beside the CEO of our media organisation on my final day with the company. Captain Mayhem handed me a pair of chopsticks.

Together with my colleagues, we boisterously tossed the ingredients in the air and wished for greater prosperity for all.

Captain Mayhem thanked us for our efforts and then went through a couple of housekeeping matters.

First, Mr Louder was now well enough to return to the Rojak Breakfast Show on Monday morning, which triggered a huge, heartfelt cheer from everyone in the office. And second, my interview with Mr Louder had been awarded the Feature of the Year prize.

THE CAREER

POST JOURNALISM

Day 1

When I woke up, I called the vice-president at Equality Matters and unloaded on the poor woman. Her kindness made me cry. She suggested that I should write a feature on sexual harassment in the workplace for their website, perhaps anonymously, which felt a little too soon and too obvious. I said I'd consider it.

I think I'll do some volunteering work with them though.

In the evening, my parents hosted a Reunion Dinner. My little cousins asked me to put on my durian costume.

I told them I didn't own a durian costume and asked them to stop playing the TikTok clip.

My inquisitive aunties explained that people are supposed to look fatter on TV and yet, amazingly, I somehow looked fatter in person.

I thanked them for their kind observations.

After our Reunion Dinner, I sat down with my parents at our kitchen table and told them I was quitting my job. I hinted at the reasons, but without giving specific examples. I didn't name names. I blamed my decision on the 'office culture'.

My father said he was ashamed of me. He said I was throwing away a scholarship and a fixed income because of some silly, feminist ideals. Then he left for the KTV lounge.

When he was gone, my mother hugged me. We sat and held hands at the kitchen table, listening to Smooth Voice on the radio.

When I was getting into bed, I got a WhatsApp message:

> 'Eh, Monkey Girl, you at home, is it? Come celebrate CNY with me *lah*.'

I liked the idea, but didn't want to go alone. I picked up the phone and hoped for the best.

An hour later, Lauren and I were running through Chinatown, giggling like schoolgirls and desperately trying to find Heaven.

Eventually, we spotted Mr Louder dancing outside, waiting for us to join him.